A FEAST FOR FLIES

LEIGH HARLEN

Dancing Star
Press

A Feast for Flies by Leigh Harlen

First published by Dancing Star Press: 2023

www.dancingstarpress.com

Cover Illustration by Vitalii Ostaschenko

ISBN: 978-1-7321418-6-5 (paperback) 978-1-7321418-7-2 (ebook)

10 9 8 7 6 5 4 3 2 1

A FEAST FOR FLIES

This book is dedicated to dogs.
Especially to Anya and Indy, truly two of the best.
You can't read this book, but you're in it.

Chapter 1

Zira already knew that Curtis Farrow was guilty. The proof was documented by pictures, DNA evidence, and the testimony of his clients and co-conspirators. More than that, he wore his guilt like a neon sign. Reeking of fear sweat, with resigned, fearful lines pinching his eyes as he shifted and squirmed in his chair, refusing to meet her eyes.

For ten years he sold false identities to those hoping to escape debt collectors, ex-spouses, and the Office of Corrections, Enforcement, and Surveillance (OCES). All that remained was the formality of reading his mind. Sometimes she could save people. Miss a detail, mitigate a sentence. But his guilt was too obvious for her to do anything to save him and trying would only get her in serious trouble.

She stroked Bea's soft, speckled fur, reluctant to release her grip on her support dog. He rested his head on her knee and whined. Dread about what she had to do soured her stomach and she tightened her grip on his long fur.

"Zira, is there a problem?" Lieutenant Paulson leaned against the locked, grey door. The harsh lights made his thin face appear cavernous and sickly.

She scowled. He'd seen her do this dozens of times in the six months since he'd been assigned as her handler. He knew full well the toll it took on her. Though, truth was, he wasn't the worst handler she'd ever had. At least he watched from inside the room instead of hiding on the other side of the two-way mirror like a child afraid of the boogie man.

Curtis' wide bloodshot eyes begged her to refuse. If only she had that option.

Zira nudged Bea's head off her knee and stroked his back one more time, taking in one last bit of quiet, and then released him.

The cramped interrogation room hummed with feelings. Paulson's irritation was like bored fingers drumming on a desk, and the terror pouring off Curtis Farrow was an icy fist twisting her insides.

Bea sensed her anxiety and tilted his blocky head, waiting for the command to provide comfort, to help her reconnect to her own feelings, and to block out everyone else's. She lifted her hand, held it flat, and pressed down telling him to stay where he was. He curled up under her chair.

"I'm going to touch your hands," she warned Curtis.

"Please, no. Don't." His scarred and meaty hands jerked against the shackles that bound them to the table.

She swallowed her fear and guilt and rested her fingers on top of his. He jolted as if she'd electrocuted him and then froze. His fear was like a pitcher of ice water poured over her brain. It silenced Paulson's thrumming impatience and threatened to flatten her own feelings under the deluge. She bit her lower lip until she tasted warm, coppery blood. The sharp pain helped pull her back into her own body.

Reading a mind was not like picking up a book and thumbing through the index to find the page you wanted. It was a labyrinth of time-addled thoughts and half-remembered memories, where connections were obvious to the one who lived them, but an incoherent, non-linear knot for anyone else.

Plus, there were the flies. They weren't real flies, that was just how she thought of them. The swarming, winged nightmares were drawn to dark memories and they clustered around them, adding yet another layer of chaos. She had no idea if they were merely a visual interpretation for what she felt when reading a mind, or if there was some deeper neuroscientific or theological explanation. She only knew that she hated them, and the way they made her feel as though her entire body was coated in thick, black, wicked oil both inside and out. But with practice Zira had learned how to sweep them away and bring the memories she needed to the surface where they could be seen, and when required, plucked out.

She activated her tablet, careful to keep one hand on Curtis' clammy skin. A picture appeared on the screen of a dark-haired woman. A white sheet was pulled up to cover her breasts, but revealed six one-inch-long stab wounds in her upper chest and shoulders.

As soon as he saw the woman, the memory clawed up from behind the squirming curtain of flies.

The dark-haired woman pounded on his door screaming, "You cheated me. You dumb fuck, you con, you piece of shit grifter!"

Curtis opened the door, grabbed her wrist, and yanked her inside hoping she would quiet down. But she didn't. She slammed her gaudy-ringed fists into his chest until he felt bruises blossoming and screamed that she'd failed the background check during a job interview at a casino, the Silver Spoon.

He tried to explain that she had paid for an ID that would stand up to a moderate level a scrutiny, enough to get her a job in retail or food service, not the kind of intensive background check required by a casino.

She threw a desk lamp at his head. He ducked, and it shattered against the wall into mint green ceramic shards.

Curtis' annoyance blossomed into rage. How dare this ungrateful bitch come to his home and scream that he was the one who'd fucked up? She was the one who showed up to work as an accountant high on stardust. She was the one who fought with him, low-balled him, berated him to get the best deal possible. Well, the best deal possible didn't buy his best work. Fuck her.

Lights turned on in the apartment across the scuffed metal courtyard. His rage took on a hot spark of panic. He needed her to shut up or someone would call OCES. He'd seen the remains of people who had faced punishment at the hands of a Reader, and the memory of their placid faces was terrifying. He grabbed a knife from his desk drawer and held it out in front of him.

"You need to shut up."

She screamed. Anger and panic swirling in his brain, he lunged. She threw her arms up in front of her face and he stabbed deep into her right forearm. She shrieked again and clawed at him as he used his larger body to barrel into her, knocking her to ground. He brought the knife down and stabbed her in the chest. He'd killed before, but never like this, never in a panic. Never with a simple kitchen knife. It was dull, but still took less force than he'd imagined. When he pulled the knife out, it caught on one of her ribs. He twisted, bone popped and crunched.

He stood and wiped his knife on his pant leg. The woman was dead. He didn't remember stabbing her so many times. His hands shook as the adrenaline wore off.

No one came. No sirens, no screaming neighbors. He didn't feel guilty about killing her. If only she'd done what he said and stayed away from high security buildings. It really was her own fault.

The memory confirmed all suspicions about Curtis. She glanced up at her handler and nodded.

"Good. Carry out sentencing," he said.

She braced herself and pulled it all out like a rotten tooth. But unlike a dentist, she couldn't throw the offending thing away. She had to keep it to rattle around in her own head forever. She shuddered at his callous disregard, his easy shifting of blame for his actions. But there was no time to analyze him. She wanted to spend as little time in his head as necessary. She swiped the screen to display the next picture and followed a bridge of murderous fear and anger to the next memory.

A chasm opened in his mind and she tumbled inside it. It wasn't empty, not really. It was like being inside a pitch-black room with a stereo set to play nothing but white noise. It smelled like rain, metal, and flowers. She had never felt a memory like it.

She glanced down at the image on the screen that had prompted his mind to go to whatever this place was. It was a surveillance photo of him standing outside the door of a stardust lounge called Euphoria. A very exclusive lounge that had private rooms and required either an obscene amount of money to have a permanent table or several months advance reservation.

Out of reflex she swiped to the next image. The room disappeared and she was back inside his memories. She'd wonder about that place later. It didn't seem relevant to his sentencing. She followed the memory to another. All the while she swallowed his feelings and memories until at last she reached the bottom. The sludge of emotions and experiences and traumas that made him the person he was. She sucked that inside herself too. Her stomach churned and her head pulsed as if her brain wanted to escape her skull.

She felt tired. Older. As if she had lived decades of his life. But the entire thing only lasted a couple of minutes. She released his hands and sat back. She took deep breaths to still her trembling. Taking in that much of someone else was a kind of shock, not unlike a major physical injury. She was cold and her brain moved slowly, still trying to sort out what was her and what was Curtis.

Curtis's now placid face was wet with tears. He opened his dark eyes which held only blank passivity.

Zira dropped her hands to her side and wiggled her fingers. Immediately Bea crawled out from under the chair and sat next to her. She wrapped her fingers in his warm fur and the world was quiet again.

"It's done?" Paulson asked.

"It's done. The file you collected on him was complete."

"Good. Were you able to pull any names?"

Zira sorted through the blur of memories. The ones most laden with fear, anger, and joy were the strongest but most were deals that had gone exactly as planned and petty crimes that left little impact on him. But as he grew more practiced, more professional he became a meticulous record keeper to protect himself against betrayal. A list of all of his clients' new and old identities was safe, accessible only to himself and his sister, another victim of his scheming and blackmailing.

Zira shook her head. She couldn't save Curtis, but she could keep some of his secrets. "No. He made a point to avoid learning his client's legal names."

Paulson glared at the empty shell named Curtis. "Bastard."

Curtis cocked his head to the side and blinked.

"Is there anyone else today?" Zira asked.

"Nah, you're done." Paulson opened the door and gestured for her to leave.

She ignored his impatience and crouched down next to Bea. He sat up so she could hug him. He smelled warm and musky and comforting. The close contact with his uncomplicated stillness pushed the violent memories further back in her mind. She stroked his ears and he snuffled her ear with a cold, wet nose. He was the only good thing to come from being sold out as a Reader by her father. As a civilian living on the Golden Nova, it was impossible to obtain a support dog without having someone turn you in for the reward money. Even non-Readers who couldn't afford a high-tech robotic assistant and had service dogs for a disability were regularly reported and had to prove they weren't Readers. The reward was just too good and people were just too shitty.

Her legs steadier and her head clearer, she stood and wrapped Bea's leash around her hand. She wasn't a technical type, so she didn't understand how it worked, but there were wires woven into the red fabric that conducted his power to calm her mind and block out the thoughts and feelings of other people. It wasn't as effective as direct touch, so some feelings leaked through, but it made it possible for her to go outside without having to either be overwhelmed by the chaotic crush of emotion or carry all forty pounds of him in her arms, so it was good enough.

She pushed open the front door and stepped outside. The washed-out fluorescence of the station was replaced by neon lights, tourists dressed to the nines, and glittery, ever-shifting billboards that flashed and beckoned, competing with one another for attention and customers. "Get Lucky at the Silver Spoon," "A Jackpot Waits for you at The End of the Rainbow Casino and Nightclub!" "Girls! Girls! Girls!" "Head up to the Stratosphere Lounge for Stardust so fine you'll never want to come back down."

A boy raced towards her, hands full of business cards covered in glossy pictures of naked people engaged in sex acts to appeal to most sexualities and kinks. He was too young to even be looking at those cards, let alone to understand the acts being performed on them. When he saw

OCES insignia on her jacket, his face went stony and he veered away.

Even without emotions bouncing around, the lights and bustle was overwhelming. Zira had lived on this ship her entire life and had no idea what possessed people to come here as tourists. But they did. In droves.

In old videos, the Golden Nova looked like a proper spaceship. A massive, hulking piece of machinery that had been built outside Earth's poison atmosphere because it was too big and too blunt to ever break the planet's atmosphere. Bare, metal walls, coffin-sized sleep compartments holding thousands of people, and wide-open windows looking out at the vastness of space. But after a plague swept through followed by a military coup, the numerous sleep compartments were no longer necessary and generation after generation of corporations and casino bosses had torn out the old and replaced it with layers of glitz made from fabrics and metal stolen and recycled from those ships whose population had been obliterated by plague or war. She imagined those abandoned bare ship skeletons floating behind them like breadcrumbs. No effort or expense was spared to allow people the fiction that this was a paradise of entertainment and decadence instead of a metal tube floating aimlessly through space.

Only one basketball-sized porthole remained in this part of the ship to see the stars. Its very existence probably the result of a small thorn of mistrust leftover from the long-settled wars that said maybe they should maintain the ability to see what the other ships were up to. She leaned in close enough to feel the cold of space radiating off the glass and gazed out at the black and the stars to give her eyes a break from the flashing lights. Ships floated nearby, a flock lost in the black. She recognized the distinctive green hull of the Oasis and the nearly invisible black Pteropodidae. Hundreds of others floated out there among the stars, allegedly on a search to find a new home planet for all their passengers, but if anyone ever thought they would succeed, they had died generations ago. Each ship its own floating nation with allies and enemies, trade partners and rivals.

Once, she had dreamed of escaping the Golden Nova for one of the other ships. On the ship-to-ship radio she kept squirreled under her bed, she'd heard there were ships out there who didn't utilize Readers at all. The Oasis was supposed to be full of trees and people who grew their own food, ate, screwed, tripped out on homegrown psychedelics, and otherwise amused themselves however they wanted while they wandered aimlessly through space like fattened, happy cows. That sounded pretty damn good.

That might have been a possibility if she'd gotten transport money together ten years ago, but now she was in the system on the Golden Nova as a Reader. If she tried to board a transport ship, the DNA scanners would clock her immediately and send an alert to Paulson and the entire OCES and they'd deny the ship permission leave until she was retrieved.

She ran her fingers across the cold glass. Bea nudged her with his nose.

"You're right, pup. No reason to waste time dreaming about might-have-beens. Let's go home."

Zira yawned and ambled to the transit station and waited

for the sleek, silver car that hung from and ran along a track the snaked along the ceiling and tucked herself and Bea into a seat in the empty end of the car.

In order to create a tense peace between the military leaders who had long ago taken control of the Golden Nova, the ship had been divided into four areas of control, each taking half of one of the two levels. Zira lived on the edge of Quadrant Four, which consisted primarily of casinos, hotels, and high-end restaurants and shopping centers. Each quadrant had its own politics and culture to some degree. One was dominated by bloodier and more violent entertainment, including greenhouses that had been converted into minuscule hunting preserves and sports of all kind that boasted no safety equipment or penalties for dirty moves. Two by black market drug production and a particularly ruthless pharmaceutical corporation, and Three held the things wealthy tourists didn't want to see: factories, forced labor housing, and trash processing.

Her corner of Quadrant Four was the Copper District and was reserved for the respectably employed but lower-class residents of the Golden Nova. Dealers at the casinos, waiters, dancers, and tour guides. It was a definite upgrade from the crowded, multi-family dormitory in the Bronze District where she'd grown up, but was a far cry from the Silver District's luxury restaurants and spacious, glittering hotels, or the Gold District and its massive, multi-floor dwellings built into the far corners of the ship for the wealthiest corporation heads.

The car hissed to a stop and she and Bea stepped out, the five-minute walk from the station to her apartment relatively quiet in this part of the ship with most of the residents at work. Her housing was typical of the Copper District. One room units were stacked and looked for all the world like massive safety deposit boxes at the bank. She rode a creaky, humming, unwalled lift from the ground up to the seventh level and stepped off onto a narrow platform in front of her door.

Her living quarters consisted of a single room big enough to hold a small kitchen, a table, a small couch, and two living room chairs. The bedroom and the bathroom were tucked into the far corner of the room, each hidden behind a frayed, red curtain. The walls were windowless, unfinished metal. She kicked off her shoes and plopped down on a threadbare loveseat with a sigh. The shaking had subsided completely, but it had left behind a ponderous sadness that leached into her bones and weighed her down.

The softness of Bea's fur and his unfailing devotion and the hopeful hum of the voices coming from the Golden Nova soothed her mind enough to unhook Bea's leash. "Okay." She snapped her fingers and his demeanor changed from serious and alert to relaxed and playful. He caught sight of his favorite toy, a bright red knotted rope. He jumped on the rope and carried it to her. Zira grabbed one end while Bea tried to pull it from her hands, growling and wagging.

Zira let go of the rope. "Oh no, you got it."

Bea stumbled backwards, shook the rope ferociously, and rolled on his back. He held the rope between his front paws and gnawed on it.

It soothed her to watch Bea relax. She didn't know what he understood about the things they did at the station, but she knew it took a toll on him as well.

When he tired himself out playing, he climbed up on her lap.

"You're much too big to be a lap dog, you know."

He licked her face, his breath pungent and meaty.

"Oh gross. I need to brush your teeth." She laughed and reclined the chair to make them both more comfortable. He rested his head on her chest and his soothing heartbeat fluttered against her stomach. With his bony knees poking her in the side it wasn't comfortable, but his warmth and unconditional desire to be closer to her eased her sadness and loneliness. After a few minutes he began to snore.

Careful not to wake him, she pulled her illicit radio out from where it was wedged between the arm of the chair and the seat cushion. There was nothing new coming through, but she let the familiar, soothing voice of a stranger, far away on the Oasis inviting people like her to come as refugees to their ship. They didn't approve of the way ships like the Golden Nova censored news and ship-to-ship communications. Claimed the way Readers and others deemed dangerous, offensive, or useless were treated on many ships was cruel, bigoted, and irrational. Between the lines, she also heard them say they needed people on the Oasis. There weren't enough bodies to plant and harvest the food or to collect waste and trash to be recycled into water and useable building materials. But that was okay by her. You didn't get something for nothing, and a safe harbor off this damn ship was a huge, important something that she wanted more than anything. Spending her days caring for green plants sounded like fucking paradise.

It was an impossible dream. She couldn't leave the Golden Nova without getting caught.

She stroked Bea's fur and imagined playing with him amidst lush green plants until she fell asleep.

Chapter 2

Zira woke to Bea's sharp warning bark. He hopped off the chair, digging his nails painfully into her stomach, and stood, hackles raised, beside her. She strained her ears to hear a faint scratching of metal on metal and then the distinctive pop of the lock. The doorknob rattled. Instinctively, she turned off the radio and shoved it beneath the chair cushion. Before she had time to stand, the door swung open and the light from the world outside temporarily blinded her.

"Who's there?" she called. The door closed and Zira blinked to readjust to the dim light.

A tall, sturdily built woman with curly black hair held a thin-bladed knife with a handle that glimmered red like a huge ruby. The kind that casino security carried clipped to their belts or in sheaths on their wrists. Beautiful enough to catch the eye and remind cheaters and thieves that those thin blades slipped easily between the ribs.

Bea growled.

"Keep your dog in check, freak." The woman waved the knife.

Zira put a reassuring and protective hand on his back. His muscles were tense and his teeth bared, but he quieted.

The stranger turned on the floor lamp beside the door and Zira recognized her. Curtis Farrow's sister. She fished around the stew of memories and sins she had swallowed that morning. Her new name was Anna Lytle and Curtis hadn't known what she did to make her want to change her name but had assumed it was criminal. But she'd gathered enough in Curtis' head to know he always assumed people's reasons were nefarious or malevolent.

Zira removed her hand from Bea's back. Fear and rage rolled off Anna and burned and clawed against Zira's chest. She could make a run for it. Try to dart past Anna or even bowl her over and race out the door. Anna wasn't a professional and she would have to be close for the knife to do her any good. But she had to worry about herself *and* Bea.

"So, you're the mind eater." Anna looked her up and down. "Did you kill Curtis?" The knife wavered when she said her brother's name and her fear increased so much that Zira could see the hungry memory flies buzzing behind her eyes.

Zira wanted to argue against being called a mind eater and to insist that Curtis was still alive. But this wasn't the time and Anna wasn't exactly wrong. "I – yes. Curtis is gone."

Relief like a cool wind followed by a hot, sticky flood of guilt. "How much did you take? Do you know me?"

Zira took a breath to calm her nerves. She needed to be able to think, but she was off-balance and groggy. She didn't know if a lie or the truth was more likely to save her and Bea.

She raised the knife and her gaze turned hard. "Answer me or I swear to god I will kill you and your dog."

Zira spoke slowly, selecting each word carefully. "I know who you are, Anna. I know Curtis blackmailed you into holding his client list in case he got in trouble."

Anna's dark eyes widened and despair swept away her rage and fear in a cold wave. "That's it then. It's over."

Zira had felt the memory of that wash of despair in many minds right before they killed. She needed to pull Anna back. "And I'm the only one who knows that."

"What?" She narrowed her eyes.

"Think of me and my job what you like, but I didn't tell anyone about you or about Curtis' client list. And I won't."

Anna licked her dry, peeling lips. "Why should I trust you to keep your mouth shut?"

Zira didn't have an immediate answer to that. She could feel a small thread of hope running through Anna's fear and desperation. Anna didn't want to kill her. Zira could work with that.

The seed of an idea began to germinate. There was no time to mull it over, so she'd have to process it aloud and hope for the best. "I can do you one better. I'll take it from you. The password, all the access details for his client list and anything else you'd like to forget. I'm good. I can be that precise. Without a handler as witness, anything I learn that I don't already know is tainted, inadmissible as evidence against you."

"You could just take everything. Leave me a drone."

Zira nodded slowly. "I could. But for one, unofficial Reading is a death sentence. It's in my best interest to not leave a drone wandering the ship, with my DNA all over her clothes and her face all over my building's security cameras." Not a bad idea to remind Anna about the cameras, if she left Zira dead on the floor, she'd be a primary suspect.

"And two, I don't want to. I don't want other people's memories clogging up my brain, it's exhausting and painful. I want to take as little of you as I possibly can. Three, it's the only idea I have that will get all of us out of here alive, intact, and out of the hands of OCES."

"What if one of Curtis' clients comes after me?"

"I'm not going to lie and say that definitely won't happen. But what good does being able to access that list do you now? Now that he's gone, his clients are more likely to kill you if you have those memories. Or hunt you down to torture the password out of you. Unless you want to force some innocent person to be your insurance policy. Do to someone else what Curtis did to you. I'm volunteering to be the last living person to know that password. My position protects me, at least somewhat."

Anna nodded her head resolutely and let the knife drop to her side. "Not many would be foolish or bold enough to fuck with a Reader. I need to think. This is big, you know? Just letting someone play around in my brain."

"I understand, but we don't have a lot of time. This building has DNA scanners and I'd rather not have you register more than once."

"Fuck. I know. I wasn't really thinking when I came here.

I heard about Curtis and just... reacted. Alright. How does it work?"

Zira's legs shook with relief and Bea's hackles lowered. She waved at the kitchen table. "Sit down. I'll answer whatever questions I can."

Anna pulled out a chair and sat. She kept the knife on the table, but her grip was loose. Definitely her first time doing something like this.

Zira sat across the table from her. Anna looked a little like her brother, mostly it was the dramatic bow of her lips and her long nose, which without the telltale lumps of multiple breaks was quite elegant. Their similarities made the scene feel uncomfortably like the interrogation room.

"What do you want to know?" Zira asked.

"What happens to us both if someone comes after you?"

"Given you did, apparently that is a lot easier than I thought," Zira forced a weak chuckle. "But I am the only Reader in this quadrant. If someone has any brains at all, they'll correctly assume that I got the password from Curtis during his interrogation. Most of them probably ghosted in hopes their IDs were still good to get them off the Nova. So, I'm hoping that taking your memory won't be putting me in anymore danger than I already am in. It puts you in a little less since you'll be able to honestly say you have no idea, even if OCES picks you up for Reading."

"Will it hurt?" Anna asked.

Zira pictured the faces of people she had read. She had no idea what it felt like for them, but she usually left her victims crying and shaking. When had she started thinking of them as victims? She'd always used the word 'targets' like her handlers told her to. She swallowed.

"I don't really know. Readers can't read each other. I don't think it hurts exactly, but it seems like it's uncomfortable."

"Why?"

"Why is it uncomfortable? I mean, I'm in your brain and pulling memories to the front that you've pushed to the background for a reason..."

"No, why would you do this for me?"

Zira squirmed. "Is my not wanting you to not slit my throat not sufficient motivation?"

Anna shook her head. "No. I mean, it is, but you were already protecting me. You could have told OCES about me. About all of Curtis' clients and saved yourself from well, me."

Zira drummed her short, bitten nails on the table. She lived with a dog and no other people for a reason. Dogs were more observant, but they didn't pry into what they saw.

"You're going to be getting real intimate with my head. Is it so much to want to know why?" Anna said.

She shrugged. "I don't think anyone deserves to get in trouble for just wanting a fresh start."

Anna searched her face and then nodded. "Fresh starts are hard to come by."

"Too hard. Any other questions?"

The corner of Anna's mouth turned up in a tired smile. "I don't think so. Let's do this."

"Is there anything else you want me to take?"

"I wish... no. I mean, there are things I'd like to forget but I shouldn't, you know?"

"Yeah. I know."

"If you take my memory, will I just have no idea why Curtis helped me?"

"Your brain will make something up to fill in the gaps. At least most people's do."

Anna took a deep breath. "Maybe I'll invent a kinder brother. What do I do?"

"Put your hands on the table. I'll touch you. It will only take a minute or two."

Anna rested her hands on the table, her fingers adorned with stylish, long black and green nails. Zira reached over and rested her own calloused, peeling hands on top.

Flies. Swirling, swarming, and buzzing. They spilled from Anna's eyes and mouth and covered her face. Zira slid through the swarm. Anna was not a violent person. She'd never held anything more dangerous than a steak knife before tonight. But she'd seen and witnessed more violence than most and for that, Zira felt kinship with her.

She'd come to Curtis begging for a new identification, a good one, one that would let her move in to her own apartment and go to school to be a nurse, even get on a transport ship if needed. An identity that no one who knew her could find. She couldn't take living with her parents any longer; the terror, screaming, bruises, and the ever present, explosive tension. So, she packed a bag and ran to her brother, even though he was a mean bastard, too. He came to the door, switchblade nestled in his palm, eyes bleary from sleep and too much alcohol, and let her inside.

"I don't work for free," he said.

"I don't have any money. But I am your sister."

He opened the door and gestured for her to leave. But then he stopped and cocked his head to the side, studying her. He shut the door and locked it.

"I got an idea how you can pay me back. I've been working on a kind of insurance policy and I could use someone who owes me."

She slumped. "You haven't changed. There's always a price."

"Well, yeah. That's life, kid. No free rides. Are you in?"

"What do I have to do?"

"Nothing hard. There are some people out there who think they'd be safer if I died and took my knowledge of who they are and who they used to be with me. I keep a list. It's well protected. High security, encryption, multiple passwords. That kind of thing. I'm going to teach you how to access it, when and if to distribute it if something happens to me. Everyone'll know I've got someone ready to send their names out to OCES or the news should I disappear or die under mysterious circumstances. But not who. Trust me, I'll make sure your new identity is good enough that no one figures out you're my sister. That's in both of our best interests. You don't gotta do anything with that list day to day, except know how to access it. And don't you dare try to play me. I'll test you, make sure you haven't forgotten. If you try to run, sell me out, or fail to remember what you need, I'll put your new ID on the fucking news. If something happens to me or if I give you the word, you post that shit online, call the news, tape it the walls. Do whatever you gotta do to make sure my threat is good. You got it?"

"That sounds dangerous," she said.

He laughed. "You're asking me to risk my own ass, kid. Besides, an ID that good costs more than you make shuffling cards at Silver Spoon in a year, so I'd call it the deal of the goddamn century."

Zira plucked the memory out and swallowed it down. Then she hesitated. Anna hadn't agreed to this part, but she saw no other choice. She swallowed Anna's memories of the entire day. She wouldn't remember finding Zira or the deal they'd made.

With one hand still wrapped around Anna's fingers, Zira grabbed the knife and slid it into the waist of her pants and prayed that she didn't accidentally sit on it and stab herself in the ass. She released Anna.

Anna opened her eyes, blinked, and looked around the room.

"Don't be scared. I brought you up to my apartment after watching you faint just outside. Do you feel okay?"

"I – yeah."

Zira feigned a dramatic sigh of relief. "Good. I don't know if you took something or if you just got low blood sugar. But you said you didn't want to go the hospital."

Anna stood and swayed. She looked frightened and Zira couldn't tell if she believed the lie or not.

Zira tried to give her a reassuring smile. "You're welcome to sit a moment. Or I can call you a local transport drone."

"No. Well, where am I?"

"About three lift stops aft of the Stratosphere."

"The absinthe bar? That's not far. I'm okay to walk home. Thanks for looking out. Not many people would bring a disoriented stranger into their home like that."

Zira smiled. "Think nothing of it. Take care and get some rest."

Anna opened the door and turned. "Your dog is so cute."

As if he knew he was being talked about, Bea leaned against Zira's leg. She rubbed his ear. "And he knows it."

Zira bolted the door behind Anna and collapsed into the armchair. She patted her leg and Bea leapt into her lap. "Thanks. You're a good pup."

Chapter 3

A day passed and Zira grew more confident that her plan had worked and that she and Anna were safe. She poured tea into a heavy ceramic mug and inhaled the scent of bergamot.

Someone pounded on the door. She froze with the mug halfway to her lips.

"Open up. Now."

She recognized Paulson's voice. There was probably someone she needed to Read. He did not find out about Anna. He did not find out about Anna. She swallowed, rested the mug on the counter, and walked to the door with Bea at her heels.

"You missed something," Paulson said as soon as the door creaked open.

"Excuse me?"

"The Farrow case. You missed something."

She hid one trembling hand behind her back and steadied the other on Bea's ever patient head so they wouldn't give her away. "It happens. What exactly did I miss?"

"His sister. He made an identity for her. Surely, he would have remembered his own sister?"

The world slowed down. Her heartbeat thrummed in her ears and beads of cold sweat popped up on her skin. How had he found out about Anna?

"You would think so. I honestly don't know what to say. How did you find out about the sister?"

"Murdered last night. Probably had something to do with his business besides just being a client, or else that's one hell of a coincidence."

Zira's stomach churned and bile burned the back of her throat. She swallowed. "What do you want me to do? I can't read the dead."

"You've had time to sort through everything you Read. Anything about his sister in there?"

She feigned being deep in thought as if flipping through the memories she'd taken. "I have memories of him having a sister. The family wasn't close or particularly... kind. But I don't have any memories of him working with her."

She braved letting go of Bea for a moment. She could tell by Paulson's face that she was on thin ice. Tendrils of fear and disgust always wove around him in his dealings with her, but were now almost palpable waves mixed with mistrust and something else. She felt it burning in his chest like heartburn. Desperation. If only she could touch him, figure out the source of his feelings. But she didn't dare. If he even suspected her of trying to Read any deeper than the haze of emotions surrounding him, he'd have her arrested.

"Lieutenant, I am a very good Reader. I don't miss much, but it is a kind of art form. Sometimes things get lost. People bury their memories or burn holes in their minds with too much liquor or stardust. Now, if you don't mind, unless you have something for me to do, I didn't get much sleep last night."

He narrowed his eyes. "There has to be an inquiry. Standard procedure when a Reader fucks up. You'll have to come and prove that your, uh, ability is still adequate to the dispensation of justice."

"Unnecessary, but I understand that procedure is procedure. Let me know when I should come to the station." She moved to close the door.

He grabbed the door and forced it open wider until she stepped back. "Today. You'll get a call as soon as they can schedule a test subject. You're on suspension until you're cleared and you're the only Reader in this quadrant. I need you back as soon as possible. Assuming you coming back is in the cards."

"Shit. Okay. Can I eat breakfast? Or would that be an imposition?" She was shaking and she couldn't tell if it was anger or fear.

"Eat fast." Paulson turned on his heel.

Zira closed the door and collapsed against it. She didn't notice she was crying until Bea licked the salty tears from her cheeks. She buried her face in his fur and inhaled. He always smelled grassy and sweet, like the inside of a greenhouse, even though they hadn't been inside one for months.

"Okay, pup, I think today is going to be rough. But it can wait until after breakfast."

Bea watched her with wide, pleading eyes. If he understood none of the other words, he certainly understood the word *breakfast*. With him following so close she nearly tripped over him, Zira scooped twice his usual food into his bowl. It was likely to be a long and stressful day for them both. She didn't know everything that went into an inquiry, but at the very least it would involve Reading someone and if she failed... well, handlers had told her on more than one occasion that a dead Reader was better than an untrustworthy Reader.

After they ate, Zira grabbed her emergency bag from the closet. It had supplies to last her and Bea a week, a small computer, and a phone her law enforcement handlers didn't know about. A habit leftover from her more mobile and less legal past. It might not be a bad idea to keep it near at hand until everything settled down.

She debated breaking into the apartment manager's office to try and delete Anna's DNA scan from the record, but Paulson hadn't come to her door to tell her about the inquiry out of professional courtesy. He could have called for that. No, he'd already have checked the record and its disappearance would look even worse. But she could erase any sign of Anna from her apartment. She set to work scrubbing down the table, the chair Anna had sat in, and the door.

As she cleaned, she tried not to think of Anna's scared face and how scared she must have been when someone killed her. Zira was fine, she was fine. She was going to get through this, however long it took, and then she could have a big, weeping, screaming meltdown when she could be sure no one was watching her for signs of instability or dishonesty.

The knife she stashed in a small safe tucked into a hole on the bottom of her mattress. It would have to stay there until there weren't so many eyes on her and she could find a way to dispose of it discretely. When she felt sure the apartment was as clean of any trace of Anna as it could be, she tried to sit down, but nervous energy sent her back to scrubbing already spotless surfaces.

Her phone chirped. The screen previewed a number but no name. Only OCES and the extremely wealthy and paranoid could have their name removed from the communication system.

"Hello?"

"Good afternoon, Zira," a cheerful woman said.

Zira said nothing while she waited for the woman to continue.

"You have been scheduled to appear for an inquiry in one hour. Please report to room twelve for testing."

"Very well."

"We look forward to seeing you."

The woman had the distinctive flattened voice of someone who had lost a chunk of memory and personality to a Reader. Zira hadn't performed sentencing on her. She must have sold some of her memories to pay off a debt. It was completely illegal of course, but OCES didn't meddle with the big corps. At least two were led by wealthy Readers and one of them, it was whispered, would pay for certain types of memories. She did her best to know as little about them as possible, but it was impossible to be completely ignorant of the practice.

Zira hung up, grabbed her bag and Bea's leash, and headed toward the station. It felt like she was walking in dramatic slow motion past the constant neon lights, sleeping drunks, and wide-eyed wealthy tourists visiting from other ships. Scaffolding lined a wall of what had once been boutique shops and before that restaurants and before that something else entirely. In the center a glowing "Coming Soon!" sign promised a new nightclub. Workers climbed ladders, working as fast as possible to complete as much construction as possible before the evening when the tourists would be dressed up and ready for a night of fun. The Golden Nova didn't acknowledge the passing of time, most things never closed and the lights never changed, but some consideration was given to the sleep schedules of those from ships that still kept to some kind business day.

The brilliant, flashing neon gave way to more subdued, but still bright lighting and the casinos and nightclubs turned into tourist bureaus and restaurants. Snuggled between a place that promised tour guides to the best food, bars, or nightclubs and a patisserie was OCES headquarters. Surrounded by all the glitter, its dull matte gray walls seemed to belong to a different world.

She climbed the stairs and walked down the long hall with its dim, buzzing lights that cast a sickly green glow on the walls.

The interrogation room smelled like stale sweat, as if the air filtration had been turned off. It probably had been. Either OCES was behind on their power bills or they thought a smelly room with thin air would be an added stressor. They weren't wrong. It felt a little like being suffocated with a gym sock, and her already triggered anxiety spiked, demanding air. She closed her eyes for a second and focused on the almost rabbit-soft fur of Bea's ears.

She opened her eyes and took in a skinny young man with glasses pushed up on his prematurely balding head. He smiled ingratiatingly. Beside him was a blond woman whose face held the unmistakable blankness of someone who had been emptied by a Reader. Zira had never been through an inquiry before, but when she had been trained, they'd used drones then too, because their memories were so few that they could be easily verified.

"Thank you for coming on such short notice," the young man said. "I am Anthony."

"I didn't have much choice, but I appreciate your time. And who are you?" she asked the woman.

The woman's face remained blank and she didn't answer.

"This is Louisa. She will be your test subject."

"Nice to meet you both, I guess. I must admit, I haven't been through an inquiry. What do I need to do?"

"It is quite similar to your exam to be licensed as a Reader. Louisa was very recently sentenced for her crimes and so has few memories remaining. You will tell me what you Read in her mind, and I will verify that what you report is accurate."

"When do I start?"

"As soon as you are ready, Zira."

Zira reached across the table and put her hands over Louisa's. Louisa didn't flinch or look frightened. Likely, she didn't even know what a Reader did anymore. What Anthony said was true, whomever she had been was gone. There weren't enough memories or dark aspects to her personality to attract a single fly. She saw Louisa turning a lever at a large factory. On the conveyor belt, plastic mugs were printed with the name of a local bar and brothel.

Louisa didn't have any memories left of what beer tasted like or what anyone did in a brothel. After her shift, she returned to a cramped dormitory with peeling lemon-yellow walls to eat bland, limp sandwiches while she talked to her roommates, all drones in various phases of building new memories. Surrounding those memories was a pure, silent void. It was similar to what was left behind when she took someone's memories, but not identical. Like putting on a stranger's shoes. Even if they were the same style, size, and manufacturer, you still knew they weren't your shoes. That unfitting strangeness reminded her of the blank space in Curtis' mind, but while that felt like white noise in an empty room, this was the silent black of an immersion tank.

Zira described what she saw while Anthony scribbled furiously.

"Very good, yes, very good. Now, please take her memories," he said.

Zira snapped her eyes off Louisa's face to Anthony. "Is that necessary?"

"You still need to show that *all* of your abilities are working. Please, take her memories."

Zira swallowed the knot in her throat and plucked the few memories Louisa had rebuilt like unripe fruit. She released Louisa's hand and sat back.

Anthony put a hand on Louisa's shoulder. "Can you tell me what you had for lunch this morning, Louisa?"

Louisa furrowed her brow. "I... lunch is the meal you eat in the middle of the day. I am sorry. I do not recall ever eating lunch." Her eyes glittered with tears.

"Do not be frightened. It is okay that you do not remember, Louisa. What about your job, do you remember what your job is?"

She looked around the room, her eyes wide and frantic like a trapped animal. "I do not remember ever having a job. Who are you people?"

"It is okay, Louisa. You are safe. We will talk in a few minutes and I will explain everything," he said.

Zira's stomach turned and guilt washed over her. "Did I pass?"

Anthony put a hand on Louisa's shoulder, and she looked up at him, hazel eyes wide and hopeful. "That is not up to me to decide. But for my part of the inquiry, you performed very well." He smiled and his face was blank and pleasant, like an actor in an advertisement for toothpaste.

A sudden bolt of understanding. "You work in the factory with her?"

"I am the floor manager, yes." He continued to smile.

Zira shuddered. That was why Anthony seemed so blank, wooden. Those who committed less serious felonies kept more of their personality and memories, but whatever was taken left them with a distinctive placidity, the strong impression that something was missing but it was hard to put a finger on exactly what. It made them just as unnerving as the drones.

"Now what?"

"I will let the desk clerk know that we have finished. You will wait here for further instructions. Come along, Louisa. We are going back to work."

Louisa sniffled but followed obediently. Thanks to Zira and this inquiry, she would have to learn all of her tasks again. She would have to start from scratch, building relationships with her roommates in the factory dorm, and relearning the names of her coworkers.

"I'm sorry," Zira said.

Louisa mimicked Zira's hunched shoulders and down-turned mouth.

"There is no need to apologize. We are happy to help." Anthony took Louisa's arm and led her from the room.

A soft rap at the door and a plump man with an orange mustache entered. He nodded. "I will need to take the dog."

Zira clutched Bea's fur protectively. Sensing her anxiety, he sat up and put his head on her knee.

"The inquiry includes you both. Just a non-invasive scan. It'll be back in ten minutes."

"I want to come," Zira said.

"Sorry. Against the rules." He grabbed Bea's leash.

Bea craned his neck to look at her and sat fast, refusing to move.

Bea whined as Zira knelt in front of him. "It's going to be okay. I'll see you in a few minutes. Good boy."

Tail tucked and his head hanging, Bea followed the man out of the room. Zira drummed her fingers on the table, trying to ignore the assault of fear, anxiety, and anger that leaked in from every corner of the station.

The door opened and Zira's heart soared and then sank when she saw it wasn't the man bringing Bea back, but Paulson.

"Where's Bea?" she said.

"Your dog will be back shortly. It's standard protocol."

"What is?"

"You missed something. Something obvious. That means either you're slipping, you're lying, or the dog is faulty."

"He's a dog. He can't be faulty."

Paulson shrugged. "The dog is a tool. Sometimes a Reader gets too close and a dog will start taking things in addition to quieting them."

"Taking things?"

"Memories. Just like you do. Maybe they learn how to do it from their Readers, nobody knows."

"I've never heard of such a thing."

"Which means what? You ever even talk to another Reader?"

Zira stared at her hands. He was right. She spent most of her youth hiding the fact that she was a Reader. The only Readers she even knew about were the ones who appeared in the news. Talia Heding and her infamous stardust empire and rarely seen face. Liam Batoc with his ostentatious casinos and smiling face all over the tabloids. She didn't like to see herself as part of some community, especially a community that included people with reputations as gruesome as Batoc and Heding.

"If that really happens, it's only because they want to save us pain," she said.

Paulson shrugged. "Read into it what you want. It's a dog. It wants you to feed it."

Zira wiped a traitorous tear off her cheek. She didn't want Paulson to know he was getting to her. His disgust and fear held a vicious edge.

"Not Bea. He hasn't taken any memories from me."

"We'll see soon enough. You'd better hope we find a flaw with the dog. If not, then that leaves you either negligent or lying."

"What happens to Bea if your tests find something?"

"Not up to me, but maybe worry about yourself."

"Why did you come in here, Paulson?"

He tilted his head to the side. "This is an interrogation, Zira. You fucked up. A woman is dead. We'd all like to know why."

"Hold up. Do you think I killed her?"

"I don't know what to think. We've worked together, what, six months? A year?"

"Eight months."

"Eight months. And I don't feel like I know you in the slightest. Anybody else here, the thought never would have crossed my mind. Maybe I'd guess you had an off day or had a bit too much to drink the night before. Unfortunate, but forgivable. But with you? Who am I to say what you're capable of? Maybe you killed her. Maybe you were involved with her and Curtis Farrow at some point. Your past isn't exactly an open book, but it's not that hard to guess that a Reader who wasn't found until she was thirty-two and who never bothered to report to us herself, probably worked with people like Curtis pretty often."

"I'd never seen or heard of Curtis before that day. You were in the room. Even if you think I could be that good a liar, Curtis would have sold me out in a heartbeat if he thought there was even the slightest hope that it might help his situation a tiny bit, and you know it."

"Perhaps. Or perhaps he was more afraid of what you'd do to him if he did. And why was Anna's DNA recorded by your building's security system?"

Zira widened her eyes and furrowed her brow. "It was?"

"It was. Care to explain?"

"Oh my god. I had no idea. Do you think I might be in

danger?" Zira put the very real fear she was feeling into her voice.

Paulson searched her face, his dark eyes narrow, disbelief curdling the air around him. But also something else, fear perhaps. Why would he be afraid?

"You're saying you have no idea why she was there?"

"I mean, I can guess she wanted revenge for her brother. Whatever she intended to do though, I never saw her. But as you've so often pointed out, I am the only Reader in Quadrant Four. If she heard that her brother had been caught, it wouldn't be hard for her to guess that I was the one who performed sentencing."

He leaned back and crossed his arms over his chest like a disappointed father trying to get her to come clean about sneaking out to a party. "You've put me in an uncomfortable position. I had hoped to clear this up easily, but this is a tangle that I don't even know where to starting unraveling. If you were normal, we'd have enough cause for suspicion to send you to a Reader, but you can't read each other, so an outsider from Quadrant Two is coming to oversee an investigation into your conduct, as well as to look into your previous Readings for any signs of impropriety. We can't spare you, but there's no choice. You're suspended until this is sorted out."

"With pay?"

He glared at her. "Without pay. Lost wages to be paid retroactively should you be cleared of any wrongdoing."

"How am I supposed to eat and pay rent in the meantime?"

"Not my problem."

Zira rubbed her temples. "Fine. Bring me Bea so I can leave."

Paulson stood. "Your dog will be back as soon as they're done with it."

As he brushed past her, his feelings came into sharp focus. A sea of revulsion and fear punctuated with glee. She considered asking what about this made him so happy, but kept her mouth shut. Whatever was going on here, she couldn't trust Paulson to sort it out. Either she'd have to hope that this outside investigator was less of a bastard than Paulson, which was unlikely, or she'd have to sort it out herself.

Shit. She *was* going to have to sort this out for herself wasn't she? But how? She wasn't a detective or a journalist. All she had on her side was a maligned ability to read minds, her moderate skills as a petty con artist, and a very good dog. But no one else was going to get her out of this. If she could prove who actually killed Anna, that should clear up any suspicion about her own involvement. If she managed that, with a bit luck and a lot of ass kissing, she might be able to get herself and Bea on probation for having missed information instead of quite probably dead for conspiracy or intentionally lying. Those were a lot of very big ifs.

The door opened and the orange-haired technician led Bea into the room. Ignoring the man's condescending snort, she dropped to her knees and hugged her dog. The world quieted and she buried her face in the long fur of his neck.

"I am so sorry, Bea, you must have been scared. Let's get the hell out of here." She clipped on the leash and hurried from the interrogation room.

On her way out of the building, she took in the averted eyes and smug smiles of OCES officers and investigators watching her from their desks as she left. Well, screw them. There was never going to be any help to be found here, she was on her own like always.

Chapter 4

Zira stepped off the lift onto the spongy gray floor of the working-class Bronze District. While matte-gray floors would always be the color of home in her mind, it had been a while since she walked on them. In the Copper District where she now lived the flooring was green in a poor attempt to mimic grass. In the Gold District where casinos and the fanciest hotels were, the flooring was glittering and gold. She preferred the gray. It was ugly, but made an excellent surface for graffiti. She paused to admire a painting of a tick wearing an OCES badge with a thin knife stabbed through its body before walking around it.

It had been three years since Zira had been inside the Purple Rose, but it was the same. Air pungent from beer and liquor, the floor sticky and her shoes made a soft pop with each step. Even the clientele was unchanged, if weathered and eyes a little more glassed over from drink and exhaustion. The dark, peeling faux-wood laminate walls stood in contrast to the bar, painted bright purple and lit with color changing lights behind the smoked glass bar top. The age-tinted familiarity brought a rush of memories and melancholy.

The bartender and owner, Marlyn "No Last Names Here," still had the same spiked multi-hued purple hair, scoop-necked black shirt, and fast, steady hand pouring out drinks to her mostly women customers. The wall behind her was decorated with pictures of women of all shapes, sizes, and skin colors in various stages of undress. Some of them were tokens of affection from customers and some were pictures of old movie stars and singers that Marlyn happened to like the look of. Zira wondered if she still scoured the thrift stores for old photos and movie posters.

When Marlyn caught sight of Zira, her face hardened and the crow's feet at the corners of her eyes deepened. Those lines hadn't been there three years ago. It seemed impossible, but not even Mar was immune to the passing of time.

Zira walked to the bar, trying to maintain her composure under the suddenly silent stares turned towards her and Bea.

"Hey, Marlyn. It's been a long time." Zira climbed onto a bar stool.

"What'll it be?"

Her voice was chilly, and Zira considered ditching this entire plan. What had made her think Marlyn would help her after what Zira had done? She rubbed Bea's ears. She needed to calm down. She didn't have any allies and she was out of other ideas. It was Marlyn or no one. She cleared her throat. "Whatever whiskey you got on special. Just a splash of water."

"Double?"

Zira hesitated. She hadn't been much of a drinker since being drafted into service by OCES. But Marlyn had always liked to say only undercover OCES and looky-loo tourists ordered a single. "Yeah, make it a double."

Marlyn poured and slammed the glass down on the bar. She turned away without making eye contact.

"Mar, wait. Can I talk to you a second?"

Marlyn leaned across the bar and lowered her voice to a raspy growl. "No. You can't talk to me a second and you lost the right to call me Mar. I can't even believe you have the nerve to come in here. And frankly, I have the right to refuse service to anyone. So, I'll let you finish this one drink, but then I better not see your face in here again."

"I'm in trouble. I need help. Or I wouldn't be here."

"Then even more reason for you to finish your drink and then get the fuck out of my bar. Your troubles aren't my problem anymore."

"You have every right to be mad. But can I explain myself?"

"Stay out of my head. My feelings are my own."

"I don't have to be a Reader to pick up on you being pissed off. Look, I know you got hurt when I got caught. Shit, so did I. It's not like I asked to get dragged into being an OCES Reader. I spent my whole life trying to avoid that. But I did get caught and that was on me. So, I stayed away to keep you safe. I thought you of all people would understand that."

"You think I'm mad about that? You can be so fucking oblivious. You *knew* you were a Reader and you never told me. I was in danger of being sentenced for helping you stay hidden every second we were together and you didn't see fit to tell me. Then you took off without a word and broke my goddamn heart. Look around this bar. You think I got any problem keeping company with people who might bring trouble down on me? No. But I got no time at all whatsoever for those who'd lie to people who trust them."

Zira looked down at the brown whiskey and swirled it around her glass. She took a sip. The cheap liquor burned its way down her throat and warmed her stomach. Her defensive anger rushed out and left her deflated and sad. "I didn't come here to fight with you. I'm sorry, Mar. Marlyn. For whatever that is worth now."

Marlyn glanced down the bar at the curious stares of her patrons. She shook her head and groaned. "I am really going to regret this, but you're attracting attention I'd rather not have. Grab a booth in back and I'll come meet you when I have time for a break. I'm promising to talk. Nothing more."

"Thank you. That's all I'm asking." Zira grabbed her whiskey and wandered to the furthest, darkest corner and slid into an empty booth. She rubbed Bea's head nervously while she waited.

Her whiskey was gone when at last Marlyn slipped into the seat across the table. "So, what is it you need? Money?"

Zira shook her head. "I – well, honestly I don't know. Information and maybe some advice. I've been out of the loop for a while."

"Why me? Why not talk to your new friends in OCES."

Zira flinched. "That's harsh. You know I got no love for them."

"I know. Goddamn, but I was angry at you for so long, but I do know that." Marlyn sighed and her anger seemed to deflate, but not disappear.

"You have every right to be mad. I fucked everything up between us. I'm sorry for that. More than anything else, I'm sorry for that," Zira said.

"Yeah, you did. You really did. Sorry your dad is such a fuck." Marlyn snorted a bitter laugh.

"Me too. For all our sakes."

Marlyn straightened up and shook out her hair as if she could shake off the past. "In the interest of moving on with our lives, I'll hear you out. But that don't mean we're okay."

"Thank you. Did you ever know a man named Curtis Farrow?"

"It really has been a long time, babe. You forget this is a dyke bar? Not a lot of men named anything here."

Zira snorted. "I didn't forget. But you're one of the only independent bars in the quadrant and he wasn't affiliated with any of the big corps so I thought he might have been in here doing business with some of your clients."

Marlyn shook her head. "One, if he was, I never got his name. Two, this place ain't independent anymore and hasn't been for a while."

Zira's jaw dropped and she sputtered. "What?"

"Talia Heding bought me out near on a year ago."

"What the hell would she want with the Rose?"

"No idea. Never even tried to set up a stardust lounge in the back like I expected. She takes a solid chunk of my profits, her agents work their deals with my customers and she keeps other corps, as well as independents, out."

"Shit. What happened? I never thought you'd sell out to any of the corps, least of all Heding."

"Never thought you'd sell out and put on an OCES badge. Lot can happen in three years."

"I guess that's true." Zira slumped in her seat. Marlyn had been a long shot, but she was her only shot.

"You really are in some trouble, huh?" Marlyn's forehead creased.

"Yeah. I don't want to pull you into it. But I need somewhere to start."

"Well, maybe I can point you in a more useful direction. I still keep my ears open. What did this Curtis do?"

"IDs. Pretty good ones too. Could even swap out DNA records for the right price."

"Shit. Guessing he got caught though, huh?"

"Yeah. He's a drone now."

Marlyn squirmed. "You the mind eater who did it?"

Zira flinched at the pejorative, but nodded.

"You didn't get anything out of him?"

"I did, but not what I need. Someone killed his sister because they thought she had his client list. Now OCES thinks I had something to do with his business and killed her myself or else I fucked up. Either way, it's a death sentence for me."

"You kept his sister a secret from OCES?"

Zira chewed her lip. It was a dangerous thing to admit, but she sensed that Marlyn was looking for a reason to trust her. "Yes. I didn't tell anyone about her."

Marlyn smiled. "I'm glad you haven't turned into a complete shit pile."

Zira laughed, relieved to feel the tension between them

start to ebb. "Thanks. Me too."

"Okay. Curtis what was the last name again?"

"Curtis Farrow. And his sister was going by Anna Lytle."

"I'll see what I can find out. Lot of folks have taken to doing their business elsewhere since they don't want to go up against Talia's corp, but I've made it clear everybody's welcome to drink here regardless of any affiliation, so more loyal customers haven't taken off completely. In the meantime, you might consider checking out the Silver Spoon. But uh, either put on some rich person drag or have someone at the Tomcat fix that boring ass haircut so you fit in with the hustlers and grifters or you'll be spotted as OCES before you make it in the door."

"Doesn't Liam Batoc own the Silver Spoon?"

"Yeah, but that playboy don't give a shit what people are selling in his casinos so long as it's not Talia's products, they pay their dues losing some money at the tables, don't cheat, and don't call his dealers out for cheating. His laissez faire ways kinda fills my old niche and it's taken a nip out of my business, but not half as much as Talia's corp does. Be careful though, huh?"

"Yeah. I will."

Things suddenly felt so familiar. Marlyn smiling across the table, her full lips painted the same black and purple as her hair, trying to keep them both out of trouble.

Zira blushed and looked down at her empty glass. It felt familiar and comfortable, but it wasn't. They were very nearly strangers now. "Thank you for the help."

Marlyn waved her hand, brushing off the thanks. "So, who's this?" She pointed to Bea who was patiently curled around Zira's feet.

"This is Bea, my support dog."

Hearing his name, Bea sat up and his tail thumped against the booth.

"Can I pet him?"

"Yeah, he likes almost everybody." Zira tapped his head, giving him permission to leave her side.

He put his head in Marlyn's lap and licked her hand as she rubbed his ears with her other hand. The emotions of the bar patrons crashed down on Zira. But it was calm, familiar in a way. Lust, depression, boredom, worry, all softened and made hazy by alcohol.

"He's really sweet," Marlyn said.

Bea returned to Zira's side and the emotional din of the bar quieted down again. "Yeah, he really is. He's the one good thing to come out of all of this."

"I guess he'd have given you away before."

She nodded. "I don't suppose you have any ideas of a brilliant cover story for him? I don't much want to be around all those people unprotected."

"You know, I always thought it was odd that someone who liked music as much as you do didn't go to more concerts. Crowds must be... shit, I can't even imagine how much crowds must suck. Well, if you go with rich person drag you might get away with playing an eccentric who won't leave her dog behind, but he's a little big and muttly for the silk and diamonds crowd."

Zira ruffled his ears and he looked up at her and his tailed thumped. "You hear that, pup? Muttly."

Marlyn grinned. "I'm sorry, Bea. I don't mean to cast aspersions on your parentage." Her face turned serious as she thought. "You know... there is a dealer out of the

Copper District named Gia who managed to get a license to have a dog. Don't know entirely how she got all the approvals for the breeding, except that it was during the script scare when all those meds got contaminated. The dog can sniff out damn near anything. Special genetically enhanced nose and bred from cloned Reader support dogs."

"I suppose that could work…"

"Don't oversell it. Get your hair fixed and uh, change your clothes. Walk in like it's nothing. Some people will recognize you, you are the only reader in the Quadrant. Some people will assume you're Gia since they've heard of her with a rough description but don't know her. But most will just ignore you if you don't walk around with a guilty look on your face like you stole something or pooped in Liam Batoc's favorite vase."

Zira put a hand over her mouth and laughed. It had been a long time since she laughed for real. When had she started covering her mouth as if afraid to let the sound out?

Marlyn glanced over her shoulder at the harried bartender who kept shooting frantic, annoyed looks in their direction. "I should get back to work. It's Rain's first day and she looks about to explode. How do I get in touch with you if I find something?"

Zira grabbed a napkin and wrote her number. "This isn't my official number. It's a throwaway phone that OCES doesn't know about. If I have to pitch it for some reason, I'll come back in."

"Still smart, Zee. Good luck."

"Thanks. And thanks for calling me Zee. No one has in a long time." Zira stood and left the dark bar for the gaudy, flashing lights outside.

As she walked, she caught a glimpse of herself in the glass. Marlyn was right, she needed to get her hair fixed. It was too short to be considered fashionable by mainstream standards and too boring for underground culture standards, so she couldn't blend in anywhere in a shady and chic casino. If she was going to get anything from people she either needed credibility or money, and her paltry savings weren't even close to being enough to bribe gamblers, loan sharks, and whatever patrons of the Golden Nova's gray economy she might need information from.

She turned off the main drag and headed down a narrow, poorly lit tubular hall that sloped sharply upwards and led to a hatch. The flooring here was shiny metal and so thin that a regular flow of people walking over it had created a bumpy, dented groove down the middle. The rickety hall was a newer addition to the ship, having been installed in the last decade or so to put a cap overtop the area where the less well-to-do and disreputable residents of the ship lived and did their business so the dingy shops and seedy people weren't visible to tourists. It also created a nice shortcut. Zira popped the hatch open and climbed the ladder down.

The businesses here didn't glitter quite so much, the walls, doors, and decor more obviously made from recycled and scrapped materials, and their signs were more opaque. Their clientele wasn't tourists; you had to know what it was you were looking for on this side of the quadrant.

The sign for the Tomcat hadn't changed since she'd last been here. Painted right on the metal wall above the automatic glass door that opened and closed with a quiet hiss of hydraulics was a lean, predatory black cat with green eyes, his back arched and claws extended as if ready to swipe at anyone who dared enter.

Zira stepped into the dim parlor. A tall woman stood behind a desk made of recycled scrap metal, a mottled patchwork of different color metals. The sides of her head shaved down to the skin to frame a cherry red braid that hung down to her lower back.

The woman ran her skeptical eyes over Zira's hair and clothes. "You lost?"

"Nope."

"We don't do..." She looked Zira up and down. "Whatever look it is you got going on."

"I'm looking for a change. It's been a couple of years since I've been in. Does Jen still work here?"

The woman nodded and relaxed slightly, but still looked suspicious. "Yeah, she does. But she's not in today."

Zira was both relieved and disappointed. It would have been nice to see Jen, but she wasn't sure how welcome she'd be and wasn't in the mood for another round of apologizing. "That's okay. I'll see whoever has time."

"Lottie's free. Go on back."

Zira went down the dark hall and into the brightly lit shop. A pungent mix of chemical fragrances tickled her nose and the air was filled with clicking scissors and the hum of razors. The walls were covered in art. Bright green, blue, and orange people with explicit anatomy but unformed faces and hair made of flowers and winged insects lounged, danced, and curled provocatively around one another.

An older woman with severe gray hair done up in dark-blue-tipped elaborate spikes appeared to be the only one not working, so Zira walked up to her. "Are you Lottie?"

"I am." Lottie raised an eyebrow. "You new to this scene?"

"Not new. It's been a couple years since I've been in."

"Well, you sure as shit let your hair go to hell in the last couple years then. Got a whole," she waved her hand in Zira's face, "uptight bank teller mom thing going on. Sit down, I'll get you fixed up."

"Is it okay if my dog lays there?" Zira pointed to a space under the counter.

Lottie looked down at Bea and a smiled tugged at her pale green tinted lips. "Yeah, of course. I haven't seen a dog in forever. My grandma had one before the restrictions. I fucking loved that dog."

Bea was definitely Zira's more popular friend.

She sat down in the creaking chair. It was strange, but pleasant to be back here. OCES had strict dress codes and there was no haircut that came out of this place that would be up to code. If she went back, she'd have to cover her head until her hair grew back in its natural color and into a regulation style.

If she went back. There was a whole lot of terror and exhilaration in that *if* and she was afraid to look too hard at a future where she was both alive and free of OCES.

Lottie didn't say anything more. She turned Zira's back to the mirror and took to shaving, cutting, and painting her hair with something cool and wet. You didn't ask for what you wanted at Tomcat's. You got what the stylist felt like doing. Showing up with a photo of a celebrity to copy would get your hair shaved off entirely and your picture on the wall of shame for a month.

When she was done, Lottie led Zira to a black, chipped sink and washed the color out of her hair, dried it, and rubbed an herby smelling product in it. Then she turned the chair around for Zira to see.

Her hair was turquoise with dark blue streaks and hung in loose waves down the right side of her face and ended in a point by her chin. The left side was shaved with three sharp lines etched into the fuzz across the temple.

A smile spread across her face. It looked great; in fact, she looked like herself again. She hadn't fully realized just how demoralizing it had been to dress and present herself in the bland, professional style she'd been forced into. Like she'd been living with some part of herself muted for years.

"Lottie, thank you. I don't know if this makes sense to you, but it's really good to look in the mirror and see me again."

"Makes perfect sense to me. I already like you better."

Zira laughed and handed Lottie $50 and didn't wait for an offer of change.

As she headed out the door, the woman at the front desk nodded. "Much better. But, lose the cardigan."

Zira pulled her sweater off, rolled it up, and started to shove it in her bag.

"I meant, like, lose it in a dumpster. You can't have that hair and that cardigan. There's a rule somewhere."

Zira laughed. She had always hated the damn thing, but it was cheap, fit the dress code, and hid her against regulation tattoos so she wore it damn near everyday like a horrid uniform.

"You know what? You're right." She tossed it in the recycling compactor where it landed amongst emptied bottles of hair dye and a rainbow clump of cut hair.

"Right on." The redhead nodded.

Zira turned and strode out. She ran her hand over the shaved part of her head, enjoying the velvety feel.

As she walked, her stride elongated and she held head higher. The haircut really did feel good, and even though everything was a fucking mess, not having to go work and Read was a huge weight off her shoulders.

The distinctive jangle of her official phone startled her. She looked at the screen, it wasn't a number she recognized. Her heart raced with anxiety. It was probably just a telemarketer. "Hello?"

"Good evening. Is this Zira?" The voice was clipped and professional.

"Who's asking?"

"I'm Inspector Deanna Parvel."

"Ah, I've heard of you. Aren't you from Quadrant Two?"

"Yes. Where would you like to meet me?"

"Excuse me?"

"I've been put in charge of investigating your conduct."

"Oh. Um. When were you thinking?"

"Now."

The Inspector was abrupt even for Zira. Maybe that was her OCES persona. It was certainly off-putting and made it hard to collect her thoughts and formulate a coherent answer. "I'm out of the house at the moment. It's going to take me some time to get back." Hopefully, Deanna would let her off the hook and schedule something for tomorrow.

"That's fine. I have transportation. Where should I meet you?"

Zira looked around. There was nowhere here that she could meet some upper class OCES Inspector that wouldn't make her look guilty. She ran her hands through her hair. That cut wasn't going to help her case, but she was on suspension anyway.

"Do you know where the Sunfish is?"

"No, but my transport computer can find it easily enough. I will be there shortly."

"I'll meet you in about forty-five minutes."

The line was silent, Deanna had already hung up.

"Well, shit, guess we better hurry."

Bea wagged his tail.

Chapter 5

Though it was late for dinner, the Sunfish was still crowded and buzzing with conversation and the clinking of glasses. Artificial sunlight streamed through blue tinted glass creating the effect of dining underwater. The entire floor was a massive fish tank. Underfoot, brightly colored, lab grown fish darted among the coral.

Zira glanced around for someone who matched her mental image of Deanna, but no one fit the bill.

A woman with long black hair and bright red lips waved at her. Zira walked to the woman's table. "Inspector Parvel?"

The woman nodded. Not what Zira had expected. Her tailored suit and loose, unstyled hair an interesting mix of feminine and masculine. Her look was not a fashionable one, hair too long, and makeup too bright, suit too boxy, but it was unfashionable in a way that suggested a contrarian taste in fashion, as opposed to being dowdy or outdated.

Zira sat down. The chairs' designer had put more thought into making it look like a massive seashell than in adequate back support and she slipped on the satiny cushion. The waiter silently brought a matching bed for Bea who happily curled up inside it like a fluffy pearl.

"I, um, got a haircut just today." Zira cringed to hear her own sputtering, flailing voice.

Deanna raised a full, artificially darkened eyebrow.

"I just – I know it's not regulation. But since I'm not working at the moment, I figured it was okay for a bit." Zira's mouth wouldn't stop, it kept spitting out excuses as if her brain's controls had been severed from her tongue.

The Inspector frowned. "I don't care what your hair looks like. Readers aren't required to follow a dress code in Quadrant Two."

"Really?"

"Really. You aren't Officers or Inspectors, why should you be required to follow our uniform requirements?"

"Oh. Well, I wish you could convince them of that here. I didn't exactly sign up to wear the black and gold."

Deanna leaned back in her matching clamshell chair. Somehow she looked comfortable. Perhaps her naturally rigid posture didn't require back support. "So I've heard."

That was a mistake. She'd let her surprise make her too honest. She cleared her throat and cast her eyes about the restaurant for a waiter, hoping for someone to come and give her even a moment's reprieve from this strange, intense woman. But the staff hurried from table to table like fire ants in their crisp red uniforms, without ever meeting her eyes. She turned back to Deanna who raised a thin, drawn-on eyebrow. She must have paid them to leave them alone. No other way would they be allowed to sit in a restaurant this expensive without ordering.

"What did you want to talk to me about?" Zira asked when the silence began to make her more uncomfortable than the thought of Deanna's inevitable questions.

"Your interrogation of Curtis Farrow. Walk me through it."

"It was a standard interrogation. I prompted his memories with pictures of some of his clients that we knew about, as well as all the standard images to prompt memories of things we might not know about. His thoughts flowed pretty freely. He wasn't a particularly complicated man."

"Start at the beginning. You came into the interrogation room and who was there with you?"

"Inspector Paulson and Curtis Farrow."

"What happened next?"

Zira described the scene and the interrogation, Deanna prompting her repeatedly with requests for more detail. It took nearly two hours, far longer than the interrogation itself.

"And you saw nothing else in his head? Nothing about Anna Farrow, also known as Anna Lytle?"

"Nothing more than what I told you."

"What else did you see?"

"Nothing, I've told you everything."

"Were there flies?"

Zira froze. She'd never talked about the flies to anyone else, didn't even know if other Readers saw them.

"Yes. There were flies."

"Would you say there were more than usual? Or less than usual?"

"More than I would expect on an average person, but not really any more or less than I would expect on someone in Farrow's line of work."

"What else?"

"There wasn't anything else."

Deanna's lips pursed. "What did you feel during this?"

Zira's cheeks burned. "It was fucking horrible, is that what you want to hear? His memories tasted like ash and I was sick for hours because it felt like I had killed six people. Is that sufficient detail for you?"

Deanna didn't react to Zira's anger. "Yes. I have worked very closely with numerous Readers and I feel quite able to judge whether you are being wholly forthcoming about your interrogation."

"And?"

"And I feel quite certain you have left things out. I watched the footage of your interrogation and what you described to me wouldn't have taken quite as long as what actually happened."

"The entire thing only took a few minutes."

"Four minutes and twenty seconds. And having sat in on quite a few such interrogations, if that was all you got from his mind, it should have taken nearly a minute less."

"This isn't a precise science and not all Readers are the same."

"That is true. And why I asked so many questions. I've known Readers who get hung up in certain memories. A special softness for memories of childhood or a particular taste for reveling in a subject's sexual exploits for instance. You don't do that, you want your interrogations to be fast. No detours during the exploration and no taking of memories you don't need. And from what I've seen of your record, what you described is very much your personal style as a Reader. So, why did this interrogation take longer than usual for you?"

Zira had prepared herself to defend her past and her professionalism. She hadn't anticipated this level of knowledge and precision about her methods.

"I – I honestly don't know."

Deanna sighed and leaned back. "I value Readers very highly. I know that some of my colleagues find you... unsettling. Distasteful, even. But you provide us with a kind of certainty that I personally take great comfort in. But an untrustworthy Reader undermines that certainty. It undermines this entire system. If we can't trust what our Readers tell us they've seen, maybe innocent people are being sentenced and maybe the guilty are escaping justice."

"I – "

"This system runs on *faith*, Zira. Not just the faith of Enforcers in their Readers, and vice versa, but the faith of people in a fair and accurate justice system. So, I really and truly want to believe you. But I don't. I am quite certain you're lying about something. What I haven't figured out, is *why* are you lying to me?"

"I'm not."

"So be it. I have no choice but to maintain your suspension and continue this investigation. Your DNA is flagged, if you leave this Quadrant or attempt to board any form of transport that would take you off this ship, Inspector Paulson and myself will both receive an immediate alert. And please note, I will take any such action as grounds for conviction. The sentence is execution. The people need to know that we take things like this very seriously. Do you understand?"

"Yes." Zira hunched and flattened into her chair. Deanna was frightening in her cold certainty.

Deanna stood. "Good. I will be in touch and I expect you to be more forthcoming with your location next time I require you."

Zira clutched Bea's fur and he wiggled closer. What was she going to do? Deanna was a hell of a lot sharper than Paulson. She wasn't just looking for witnesses and evidence, she seemed to have more knowledge about how Readers operated than even Zira did.

Conviction looked a lot more likely. Poison injected into her arm and her body cut up in the name of research. Quite probably Bea, too. A bonded support dog was of no use to anyone else.

Bea whined and licked her hand, helping to bring her back into the moment. One thing at a time. Prove who killed Anna. It wouldn't end the suspicions building up around her, but it might quiet them enough. After that, she'd keep her head down, do her job, and maybe she'd get through this.

Chapter 6

The Silver Spoon was a glittering, swirling cacophony. Fast upbeat music punctuated by the clanging of coins spilling from slot machines and shouts of delight and frustration. Huge screens advertised everything from dinner to sex to the most extreme free-for-all fights. Everything was silver and gleaming. The tables, the walls, the glasses overflowing with booze, and the scant costumes on the young, smooth-skinned hosts as they refilled drinks, hung on the arms of the winners, and whispered in the ears of the losers to give it one more try, promising them that their luck was just about to change.

A handful of people glanced up from their games and their business deals at Zira and Bea. A few faces flashed recognition, hardened in suspicion, but most paid them little mind. She felt at home in her fresh haircut, but less so in heavy silver eyeshadow and lipstick and a fitted purple suit, topped off with a silver ascot that Marlyn had left in the back of her closet years ago. Still, she had the feeling like someone was watching her. She glanced around the casino and for a second thought she caught someone's eyes near the blackjack table. But when she scrutinized the crowd, there were no furtive or overly interested faces. She rolled her shoulders, the incessant staccato of emotions beating at her was probably making her anxious. She rubbed Bea's ears and her stomach settled and her heart slowed.

A woman with ringlets of artificial silver hair spilling out of a stylish and elaborate up-do approached with a liquid stride that seemed impossible on her metallic stilettos.

"Welcome to the Silver Spoon, can I get you anything?" The bright lights flickered off the silver glitter coating her eyelids and liberally dusted on her shoulders, breasts, and stomach.

"Perhaps. Have you ever met a man named Curtis Farrow?" It was unlikely that one of the hosts would have known him, certainly not by name, but there was a chance her inquiry might get to the right ears.

The host pasted on a wide, toothy smile. "The name doesn't ring a bell. But I would be more than happy to a leave a message with reception so your friend knows where to find you."

"No, that's okay. Thanks, though."

The host's glittering smile widened until it contorted her pleasant, pretty expression into something more like a pained grimaced. "Sure thing. Let me or another host know if you would like a drink, or if you would like some help learning your way around any of the games." She strolled away, her gait faster and not as seductively fluid.

Zira wandered through the glitzy crowd until she found a dark bar tucked in the back corner of the casino. This was what she was looking for. The patrons weren't tourists, playboys, and thrill-seekers losing their money at the tables. Here the clothes were functional and sleek; black was more fashionable than silk ties and heavy jewelry. It was good she'd gone to Tomcats, her new haircut fit in here much better. Although there were a handful who dressed more like the fashionable wealthy patrons outside, only a poorly tailored jacket, an ill-fitting shoe, or a ring just a bit too big to hide that it was made of glass gave them away. Probably middlemen playing dress-up to make their wealthy clients more comfortable.

She sat down at the bar and ordered a drink. While she sipped, she absentmindedly stroked Bea and scanned the room for familiar faces, but these were all strangers. A tall, thin man in an expensive, crimson-fringed jacket stood outside the bar and glanced furtively at the people inside until a green-haired woman rolled her eyes and went to speak to him. The woman looked familiar, and it took Zira a moment to realize it wasn't her own memories, but Curtis's that were triggering her déjà vu. They hadn't known each other, but he'd seen her here in this bar.

The woman and the furtive rich man made a quick exchange of money for a discrete package no bigger than a deck of cards that the man shoved into his pocket before slinking away, glancing over his shoulder at the unsmiling security guards. There was very little prohibited on the Golden Nova, he must have come from another ship where whatever he was buying was illegal.

"Tourists," the woman snorted as she returned to her table.

There were so many people here and Zira had been out of the loop so long. She had no idea where to start. A sharp pain in her finger alerted her that she was biting her nails again. She wrapped the hand around her drink. For a moment, she released Bea. It was almost impossible to get a reading in the casino. Greed, elation, rage hung heavy in the air. But in her immediate vicinity, suspicion was swirling. People were starting to take notice of her. Sharp glances and huddled whispers that stopped when she looked at them. She needed to make a move.

She stood and walked over the green-haired woman. At least she must have been aware of Curtis. "Buy you a drink?"

"You shopping for sex or snitches?" The woman's eyes were hard, and her lips were pursed so tight that they looked like a raisin.

"None of the above."

"Uh huh."

"I just want to ask you a few questions."

"You think a little hair dye is enough to cover the stench of OCES? The one and only mind-eater around here can't blend in that easy. Buzz on home."

"I'm trying to find someone who knew Curtis Farrow. He's gone. Caught, convicted, sentenced. No one to sell out. And unlike that tourist, I know selling stardust ain't illegal and I wouldn't give a fuck if it were."

The woman's face drained of color. "I don't know what you're talking about."

There it was. It was a lucky guess, but Zira had read the woman's intentional, cocky casualness correctly. Stardust wasn't illegal, but selling Talia's products in Liam Batoc's casino was dangerous.

"Besides, I don't have to be nice. I could just take whatever information I want." Zira touched the woman's hand and saw a quick flash of flies. She hoped the woman agreed to talk to her. She didn't think she could go through with that threat. But she was in a casino and she was on a lucky streak so far.

"What do you want to know?" The woman leaned forward and put her hand near her mouth to block anyone on the other side from seeing that she was talking to Zira.

"My offer was sincere. I'll buy you a drink. It'd probably look less suspicious if we're two people sharing a beer instead of one person drinking and the other looking like she's being interrogated. What'll you have?"

"Beer. Golden Hops."

Zira ordered the beer and refreshed her whiskey. The bartender placed a brown bottle with a smiling gold rabbit on the label in front of the green-haired woman. He quickly walked away, experienced enough to recognize a conversation he didn't want to overhear.

"So, Curtis Farrow. Did you know him?"

"Yeah, I knew him. He was here pretty regularly. Usually kept my distance. Not a nice guy."

"What else do you know about him? I know who he was and what he did. I don't know what people might have thought about him. Grudges, enemies, allies, that kinda thing."

"Curtis was independent. Not all the corps like that. More than a few people would have preferred he take their old names into the incinerator with him. In fact, this bar is a bit emptier since you sentenced him. Lot of people assume OCES is out looking for them. Funny though, there haven't been any arrests yet."

"Yeah, hilarious. I know all that. I need something more specific and less obvious."

The woman took a long drink of her beer. "Okay, look, I don't know much about his business, but there were some rumors. Curtis wasn't as independent as he claimed to be."

Zira raised an eyebrow. There hadn't been any memories of affiliation to any of the corps in Curtis' mind.

"There was a fight outside the Silver Spoon. Some of Talia Heding's people showed up and naturally Liam didn't put up with that. When it was over, quite a few folks were gone. It was hard to tell if they took off on their own or ended up in the back of one of Talia's transports. Curtis was one. He was a little weird after that. Forgot people's names or came in and didn't remember being here the day before. Honestly, I figured it was the booze. Man drank a lot. But some people said Madame Heding got into his head."

That weird, dark room in Curtis's brain suddenly made sense. It was the footprint of Talia Heding removing Curtis's memories.

"Anything else?"

The woman shook her head.

"Anyone who might have known Curtis better who hangs out here?"

The woman stood so fast she knocked her stool over.

"What–" Zira said.

"Please, come with us." A square jawed man with a telltale earpiece and a collection of thin, silver handled knives strapped to his belt stood behind her.

"Have I done something wrong?" Zira slid off her stool and wrapped Bea's leash around her hand.

Another stony-faced security guard appeared on Zira's other side.

"Please, come with us," he said again.

Both guards were wearing silver gloves that matched the buttons on their black uniforms. Just ostentatious enough that they didn't stand-out for being too dull in the glittering casino. But those gloves meant they knew who and what she was and came prepared. Unless she was going to jump and grab them by the chin, there was no visible skin for her to make contact with.

"Certainly." Zira tried to sound unconcerned, but her mouth was dry and her tongue heavy.

She followed the two guards through the averted eyes in the bar and the gawking stares of the gamblers on the main floor into a cramped elevator that had no buttons and felt like a silver-plated casket.

The elevator opened into an opulent suite. The furniture was rich reddish wood and the upholstery was deep crimson. Gold framed paintings of full-bodied nude women lounging languidly on pillows or amidst lush green flowers decorated the walls. The room was not as glittery as the casino, but no less ostentatious.

In the center of the room, was Liam Batoc. His face was splashed across advertisements all over Quadrant Four, and probably the rest of the Golden Nova and other ships, telling people to come to his casinos. He matched the room in a crimson suit that was closely tailored around his shoulders and thighs and then billowed out in the back. The faux cape was all the rage. Or so the style mags said. She'd never actually seen anyone wear one before, outside the glittery, shifting images on the supermarket e-reader stands. His black hair swept across the right side of his face, cut at a dramatic angle so the tip brushed his chin and the back grazed the tip of his ear. Just enough taken from places like Tomcat's to make him stylish and edgy without looking entirely disreputable. At his side sat a regal black dog with long flowing, impeccably groomed fur, and adorned with a silver collar.

"Ah, Zira. I'm so glad you decided to join us."

Zira bit back that all too obvious reply that she wasn't here by choice. Liam seemed to fancy himself a character in a film. Much more glamorous than the reality of being a leech who fed on people's despair and boredom.

He stepped to the side to reveal someone slouched on the sofa. The man's familiar bald head was buried in his hands and his scuffed shoes tapped the floor.

Zira was not surprised to see her father in Liam's casino, but seeing him in this suite was a shock. It had been three years since she'd spoken to him and time had not treated him kindly it seemed. There was a new nick in the cartilage of his ear and his eyes were almost lost in the dark, sagging circles surrounding them.

He nodded and gave her a weak smile. She ignored the gesture. Instead she stroked Bea's fur and turned to Liam.

"What do you want?"

His face twisted in an exaggerated grimace. "So abrupt. We are both Readers here, comrades of a sort. Have a seat. Catch up with your father. I'll get us drinks." He snapped his fingers and the wall behind him slid open to reveal a bar. Everything was rounded, curved, and silver, and it seemed to fit the glittering modern style downstairs better than the faux antique vibe of the suite.

"I'm not interested in catching up." Zira turned towards the door, but the two blocky security guards glowered down at her.

"We have so much to talk about. Quentin here has worked for me for so long he's practically family. It pains me to see my family so estranged. Sit down." His smooth voice took on a cold edge.

"Fine." Zira plopped down into a massive red chair that turned out to be extremely uncomfortable. The plump cushions that looked so opulent scratched her bare arms and there was something hard digging into her lower back. Bea sat between her legs. He sniffed the air and snorted at the smell of the other dog, and she stroked his head to soothe them both.

Zira and her father said nothing. Her father buried his face deeper into his hands. She stared at his pitiful form, unsure what she felt for this man who had done little more for her growing up than send the occasional check, and show up once every few months to profess his sorrow and vow that *this time* he really was done gambling and he was going to stay with them. If only her mom could lend him a little money to pay off a debt.

Liam hummed while mixing drinks, ice clinked against glass and liquor splashed. He carried a silver tray and set it gently on an ornate, dark wood table that looked like some fine antique, but now that Zira was closer, she saw the plywood and peeling paint.

He placed two cocktail glasses on the table and a shallow silver dish of water in front of Bea and took a seat across from her. "Well now. I understand you've been asking after the late Mr. Farrow."

It seemed letting that bit of information climb the grapevine to see what shook loose worked better than she'd wanted it to. "Yes." No point in denying it now.

"Mr. Farrow was caught and sentenced for his crimes and presumably, you took whatever information he had in his mind. What could you possibly hope to find out by harassing my patrons?"

"Someone killed his sister and I think it had something to do with Curtis."

Liam drummed his fingers on the plush velvet arm of his chair. "Certainly, a lot of feathers were ruffled after you sentenced him. There aren't many crimes on the Golden Nova, but the cardinal rule is that one must be identifiable and locatable, and Curtis broke that rule in as many ways as one can. I would think the people most likely to be angered by his crimes would be OCES and his own clients. The rest us of are quite content to live and let live. So, why are you investigating him here?"

"Well, the Silver Spoon is one of the few places that independents like Curtis are able to operate."

"And who says Mr. Farrow was independent?"

"He did."

Liam sighed and reclined in his chair. "I'm going to let you in on something, give you a peek behind the curtain, if you will."

"Okay. I'm listening."

"I am quite certain that Mr. Farrow was an agent of Talia Heding."

"I've heard the rumor, but haven't seen anything to prove

it," she admitted.

"Yes, well, that witch is tightening her hold all over this quadrant. She's clever, I must give her that." His eyes lost focus for a moment and he appeared lost in thought. His gaze sharpened and refocused on Zira. "She uses those like Mr. Farrow to blackmail people into working with and for her. He was of course, a bit player, but you can imagine that she could gain leverage over quite a few well-placed people who didn't want the secret of their past lives revealed to the wrong people."

The blank space in his memories must have been his meetings with Talia. She took just enough that he didn't remember her and thought his secrets were still safe, without touching any of the peripheral memories. If it was true, she was an incredible Reader. Way better than Zira.

"I can see how that would be... advantageous for someone like her," Zira said carefully. "But why are you telling me all this?"

"First, let me tell you a story."

"Seriously?"

Liam's mouth twisted in a smirk. "Seriously. Some years ago, a very loyal employee of mine, Quentin here in fact, let it slip in a haze of stardust, that his daughter was a Reader. Now, this was before Talia Heding moved in and I was quite happy being the only Reader in the quadrant. Went to great lengths to make sure it stayed that way. Frankly, we'd all be better off and this Quadrant more stable if I had succeeded. But I digress."

It was true that there hadn't been a Reader in this quadrant in some years. Less than half a percent of all people on the Golden Nova were Readers, but on a ship of a quarter million people, they weren't unheard of. Except in Quadrant Four. It was why OCES put such a high bounty on them. Was that because Liam killed them all?

"I told Quentin I wanted to meet his remarkable daughter, perhaps see if she'd work with me. He was practically family, after all. But he went and sold her out to OCES. I was not at all happy with him."

"I wasn't thrilled with him myself."

"I tell you this only because I'm making you an offer and I want to be perfectly clear." He drew a long, thin, pearl-and-onyx-handled knife from his jacket. "I want Talia gone more than anything. I'm done with her poaching on my business and killing my employees. I don't want to hear ever again that one of my suppliers is now working exclusively with her because of some dirty secret she wormed out of them. And you are going to help me do that."

"Excuse me?"

"Talia has more ties to law enforcement than I do, but most of that is in her home, Quadrant Two. Here, OCES might as well be its own corp. You and I are forming an alliance and you're going to use whatever access and power you have to help me destroy her."

"And if I don't?"

He stood and walked to the sofa where her father sat. He leaned down and tapped the blade of his knife against her father's cheek and a trickle of blood appeared, dribbling down to his jaw. "Quentin sticks close to me these days. Though I'm sure you have plenty of ugly feelings about him, you should know that in selling you out to OCES, he probably saved your life. And if you let me down, I will kill him. And if you still prove difficult, I'll kill your dog. I'll kill your ex-girlfriend, what was her name again? Ah yes, Marlyn. I'll kill the old lady who lives next door and gets your mail when you work late. I will kill every person you've ever spoken to. Do you understand?"

Zira swallowed, the sudden display of violence left her shaking. She couldn't read another Reader, but if she could, she was sure Liam would be dripping with black flies.

"Do you have some idea of where to start?"

"Yes. I'm quite certain she'll reach out to you now that you're in something of disrepute with OCES. She does love to collect Readers. When she does, you do whatever you have to do to gain her trust and report back to me anything you find out."

"I'll do what I can." Just take down the most terrifying and powerful drug lord on the Golden Nova. The odds of her surviving this whole mess were getting slimmer by the day.

Liam flashed that aces-high smile. "That's what I like to hear. Come now, you must finish your drink. I fancy myself quite a good bartender. Many of the recipes they use downstairs are my own."

The bizarre shift in mood was disorienting. Zira sipped her drink. It was good. Whiskey base with a hint of fruit, and an herb she didn't recognize. When she finished he led her, still smiling, back to the elevator and his guards escorted her and Bea out of the casino.

Chapter 7

Zira sat on the edge of her bed and yawned as she scratched Bea's shoulders. He grunted happily and leaned against her leg. She basked in the hazy warmth of just waking up in the quiet of her apartment. No flashing lights, clanging slot machines, or wild emotional highs and lows of gamblers pinging against her mind.

Her phone chirped and she groaned. Bea looked up at her with wide, doleful eyes when she stopped petting him to grab the phone from her nightstand. But it wasn't her regular phone that was ringing, it was the one she kept secret from her OCES handlers. She dug through her bag and pulled it out. Marlyn's name flashed on the screen. Her heart jolted.

"Hello?" she said.

"Zee, it's Marlyn."

"What's up?"

"Can you come to the Purple Rose? I have something for

you." Her voice was strained and tight.

"Are you alright?"

"Yeah, I'm aces."

"Sure. I'll need to take the lift, but I can be there in an hour."

"Great, see you soon." Marlyn hung up.

Zira dumped food in a bowl for Bea who more or less inhaled his breakfast, grabbed her bag, and headed out. The lift was right on time and the glass walled platform hissed down to the stop. A handful of people got off, but the lift remained crowded. The passengers who were from the Golden Nova saw Bea and gave them both a wide berth, while tourists cooed at how cute he was.

A tall woman leaned down to pet him.

"Don't," Zira snapped.

The woman jumped back as if struck and Zira felt guilt quash her irritation. "Sorry, but he's a working dog."

"Oh, um sorry." The woman frowned and scrutinized her as if trying to decide just what was wrong with Zira that she needed a support dog and Zira's irritation won its battle with guilt and she shot the woman a cold, unfriendly stare until she looked away.

The lift hissed up and flew along the track over the buildings and people below. At passenger commands, it detached and floated between decks, dropping people at casinos and hotels with exclusive entrances above the bustling crowd below. When it was almost empty, it zoomed away from the tourist-friendly areas of the Golden Nova and towards the Bronze District. and settled in a groove beside a restaurant that smelled like eggs and barbecue sauce.

When she arrived at the Purple Rose, it was still too early to open for business and inside it was dark and the chairs were still stacked atop the tables.

"Marlyn?" she called from the doorway. When she didn't get an answer she went inside.

The lights turned on to reveal a broad-shouldered woman with black hair in a tight bun sitting in a booth.

"Zira. Please, come in."

"Where's Marlyn?"

"I asked her to leave us alone for this conversation." The strange woman waved at the empty seat across from her.

She could turn and leave, no one was blocking her exit. But where was Marlyn, and was she safe? At the very least, after everything, she owed it to Marlyn to make sure she didn't get in trouble because of her own mess. She crept to the booth, Bea's leash gripped tight in her hand, and alert for any sound or sign of a trap.

The stranger had the blackest, most intense eyes she'd ever seen, and Zira had the uncanny feeling that this woman could see inside of her. As she got closer, she saw that the woman's plain black suit was actually quite fine. It was slim and tailored to the woman's body and accented with onyx and pearl buttons. She reminded her a little of Deanna. And at her feet was a dog that very much resembled a fox, the leash connecting them black and made of the same material as the leash Zira held in her own hand. Another Reader.

"Thank you for coming, Zira. My name is Talia."

Zira felt as though a fist clamped down on her lungs. "Talia Heding?"

She nodded.

Shit. Not good. This was definitely not good. "What do you want?"

"I thought it was about time we met. Please, sit down."

"I'm not doing anything until you tell me where Marlyn is."

"She's quite well. Waiting in my personal transport in fact, for us to be done with our little meeting. I'm sorry for the secrecy, but as I'm sure you can understand, I prefer to keep my comings and goings quiet." She had an odd, very precise manner of speaking as if she took the time to carve and perfect each syllable before letting it pass her tongue.

"What could you possibly want to talk to me about?"

"I have a lot I'd like to talk to you about. You're a Reader, like myself, and I take a great interest in people like us. We're a rarity. And unlike all the glittery bullshit that residents and visitors to this ship prize so highly, it's a rarity that is actually valuable. Now. Sit." Her voice turned biting and dangerous.

Zira sat. She patted the bench next to her and Bea jumped up beside her and rested his head in her lap. She couldn't quite explain it, but she didn't want Bea to be too close to Talia's dog any more than she wanted to get too close to Talia.

"I like Readers. I like to surround myself with people like us. You know what I call non-Readers?"

Zira shook her head.

Talia smiled. "Books."

Zira searched her brain. "Like in the old films and e-stories?"

"Yes. Big, heavy, paper bricks we used to write our stories in. You know why I call them that?"

"Because they can be Read but can't Read anyone else?"

She smiled like a proud teacher. "Correct. And because they're obsolete. They have the gall to think we should be in service to them."

"Uh huh." Zira had no idea what to say to this woman. She'd had ugly thoughts about non-Readers over the years. Their prejudice and fear made her life shitty. But, even if she weren't a Reader, growing up poor on a ship obsessed with wealth had made her life shitty, and Talia profited off that as surely as any other drug lord and casino tycoon.

"Perhaps even worse, there are Readers like Liam Batoc," she spat his name out like she eaten something disgusting. "Pitiful excuses for Readers want to be king of an ant hill with no other Readers to challenge him. I understand you met with him."

There was no point in lying so she nodded.

"And he wants you to come after me. To use your own considerable skills as well as your ties to OCES." She threw her head back and laughed. "That man. So arrogant."

"He said he'll kill Bea and Marlyn. And my father," she added.

"Marlyn is under my protection. He'll do nothing to harm her. You and Bea could be as well." She reached down and caressed her own dog's head with well-manicured black nails.

"And my father?"

"Your father sold a Reader out to OCES. I take great exception to that and have a mind to kill him myself. But he has proved himself useful and I keep my assets alive. How do you think I knew the details of your conversation with Liam, after all?"

"My father is working with you, as well?"

"He is. Though he doesn't know that, of course."

"Like Curtis Farrow was working for you but didn't know it?"

She smiled and nodded as if Zira was a child telling her that she got all of the words right on her spelling test.

"What do you want from me? To go after Liam?"

"Oh no, nothing so ambitious. Law enforcement in this quadrant has proved to be more difficult to deal with than elsewhere. Your OCES has too much power and too many resources to be as easily bribed and thoroughly infiltrated as in other quadrants. I was prepared to deal with Liam and any other corps that might pop up in the vacuum when he fell, I wasn't quite prepared for OCES to effectively be its own corp. And an entrenched one at that. Quadrant Two's OCES was not nearly so well-funded or influential."

"Why bother with Quadrant Four then?"

Talia leaned close. "Because Quadrant Four is where the *real* money is. Believe me, I'd have much rather stayed in Two. I've been here only a few short years and already I hate this quadrant and its circus of opulence and debauchery."

"You want me to be your spy in OCES?"

"I want to teach you how to use your ability more efficiently. You are uniquely well situated to bring me information, create spies, and make troublemakers a little bit more compliant."

"They think I might have killed someone or at least intentionally obstructed an investigation."

"Those things can be righted easily enough."

It clicked. "You set me up?"

Talia shrugged. "I took advantage of an opportunity."

"Why would I work for someone who did that to me?"

Talia leaned across the table, her electrifying black eyes locked on Zira's face and sent a jolt through her stomach. "Because I have other uses for Readers. Uses that you would like a whole lot less."

Zira wanted to ask what those were, but she probably really did not want to know.

Talia smiled suddenly. A cheery, almost childish grin that somehow even more terrifying. "Tell you what, Zira. To show you that I'm a reasonable person, I'll give you twenty-four hours to think it over. I'm also prepared to offer you a very significant amount of money. Call it a signing bonus." She pulled a plain white card out of her pocket and handed it to Zira. "Call me when you're ready."

"Come, Calypso." Talia stood and her dog trotted after her.

Zira paced the floor, her shoes sticking and popping off the bar floor with each step. This entire situation was getting more and more out of hand. She was now what, a triple agent? Spying on Talia for Liam, OCES for Talia, and investigating everyone on her own behalf in a desperate bid to not be murdered by the pack of extremely ruthless wolves surrounding her. And where the hell was Marlyn? The Purple Rose was supposed to open in an hour.

The front door chimed as it opened and Marlyn stood in the doorway outlined by flashing red and orange lights from the billboard outside. Her face a touch gray and her hair disheveled, but unharmed.

"Zee, you're all right."

"And you? You're okay?"

Marlyn nodded. "She scared the shit out of me, but she didn't hurt me."

Relief washed over her and was followed by a sudden flash of anger. "What the hell? You sold me out?"

She held up her hands. "I'm so sorry, Zee. I didn't tell her you came to see me. She just... knows stuff somehow. I tried to warn you."

"What? When exactly did you try to warn me?"

"Really? When have I ever said the words 'I'm aces?' I couldn't exactly say, 'I'm being held by a deranged Reader and she's threatening to suck my brain if I don't call you, so it'd be great if you showed up and got me out of this, but maybe be careful.'"

Zira dropped into a bar stool. Her fear was making her angry at Marlyn who she wasn't angry with at all. "Oh. That was a weird thing for you to say. I'm sorry, I got you into all this and now I'm being an asshole."

Marlyn sighed and poured them both a double. "I'm sorry. I should have been a bit more upfront about just how deep the pile of crap I'm in with Talia is."

Zira sipped her whiskey. "Okay. How deep?"

"Talia... she does this thing where she gives you just enough rope to hang yourself and then makes sure someone is standing by to take pictures."

"I've heard that. What's your rope?"

"I lied to you, before. I knew who Curtis Farrow was."

Zira frowned and then it dawned on her. There were technically many crimes on the Golden Nova. The factories were hungry beasts that needed drones. But Quadrant Four operated a bit differently. If you had money, there were only three unforgivable sins. Hiding a Reader, hiding yourself, and manufacturing projectile weapons. Marlyn was neither a Reader nor an arms manufacturer. "You had him make you a new identity?"

"Partially. OCES has been taking a bigger and bigger chunk out of independents in the form of liquor and drug licenses. I couldn't keep up, so I tried to arrange a sale of the Purple Rose to a fake identity. He told Talia, or she sucked it out of his brain, either way, she found out and tipped off OCES. In the process it came out that I knew you and that added on suspicions that I'd purposefully kept you hidden."

"I'm sorry."

She shook her head. "Don't be. I mean, I would have been real pissed at you if that's what got me in trouble, but that was just icing. Talia took care of the licensing and OCES mysteriously found some evidence that proved I hadn't known what you were, and then I was back in business with a scary-ass, mostly silent, extremely greedy business partner."

"I think she set me up for Anna's death."

"Probably."

"So, I'm fucked."

"What does she want from you?"

"Wants me to be her pet Reader inside OCES in exchange for making all my problems go away. Meanwhile, Liam wants me to take down Talia or he'll kill my dad, Bea, you, and anybody else who might have ever so much as smiled at me on an elevator."

Marlyn laughed, a harsh bitter sound. "What a mess. God, I hate this fucking ship."

"What if we left?"

Marlyn raised one eyebrow.

Zira sighed. "I mean, I know we can't. But I still have that little radio you gave me. Sometimes, I listen to the broadcasts from the Oasis and think... maybe. It's stupid. The second I try to step on an off-ship transport OCES gets an alert and I'm sure Talia, possibly Liam, have similar arrangements with Intership Taxi."

"It's not stupid. Though it would take a lot of money and someone with Curtis Farrow's skills. Plus something big, something distracting enough that they'd all have better things to do. Hm. I don't suppose having his memories is the same?"

"I know a lot more about building fake identities than I did before, but no. Sorry."

"It was a thought." Marlyn drummed her fingers on the table and looked deep in thought.

Zira cleared her throat. "Talia gave me a day to decide if I'm working with her willingly or unwillingly. I don't think Liam expects me to have taken her down that fast and hopefully OCES will still be doing an investigation and aren't currently planning an early morning execution. I'm going to keep digging in hopes of getting out of this in something like one piece."

Marlyn smiled. "I'm in."

"What?"

"You heard me. I want out of this deal with Talia and I figure you're my best shot to either get out of this or get the hell off the Golden Nova."

"Are you sure about that? It's going to be dangerous."

Marlyn chuckled. "Just like old times. Requires a little more finesse than flashing my cleavage while you cheat rich tourists at poker, but I think we can do it. Shit. You know, it just occurred to me, that's why you were so good at poker."

Warmth filled her at the memory. "And you always managed to fuck up casino security afterwards just enough so that we didn't show up on video. We were a good team. But you're right, this will be a lot harder. I think we might have a chance though. Partners?" Zira reached across the table. Marlyn hesitated a moment, but reached out and shook her hand. The warmth of Bea's head in her lap kept Marlyn's feelings and memories away, but Zira's own were powerful enough. She squeezed Marlyn's hand once and let go, her cheeks warm and her stomach fluttering.

"I'm sure Talia has ways of keeping tabs on her businesses, so I need to open the bar and keep up appearances. Can I come by your place after I close?"

Zira stared at her in surprise. "I – yes, of course you can." She scrawled her address on a napkin and slid it across the table.

Marlyn took the napkin and shoved it into her pocket. "Don't look so shocked. I meant it that we're in this together."

"Thank you." Zira suddenly felt that just maybe, she might get out of this mess alive.

Chapter 8

Zira strolled through the familiar gray halls and up the rickety stairs to the elevated walking paths of the Bronze District on her way home. The smell of spices and bread baking, the sharp-edged colorful fashion, and the cool nods of acknowledgement from the passersby. At home, everything was fake green grass, metallic and soft neutral clothing, and averted eyes. She missed living here.

Her skin prickled and she had the feeling, as she had in the Silver Spoon, that she was being watched. She slid Bea's leash up her arm so that it looped over the black and green sleeve of her jacket, cutting her off from his calming quiet. The itch of someone's anxiety over money, the foggy warmth of someone blissed out on stardust and music pouring through their headset, prickles of irritation that the lift was late, and a cold blast of someone calm and watchful. She searched the crowd but couldn't place a face with the feeling. But she was definitely being watched. Someone belonging to Talia, Liam, or OCES? At this point, it was anyone's guess.

She dropped the leash back into her hand and the emotions roaring through all around her returned to a muted, dull hum. She made her way to the lift and waited for it to descend with a small group of locals who shifted to be as far as possible from her and Bea, but otherwise paid them no mind. A quick scan of the emotions of the group milling about the stop confirmed that none of them were the one watching her.

At last the lift hissed into place in the square groove in front of them and they boarded. The lift got fuller when they hit the mid-quad Gold District stops, but it was still early and most of the tourists were either already perched in their favorite casinos or luxuriating in spas and swimming pools before whatever escapades they had planned for the night.

The lift stopped near her apartment and she squeezed through a clump of tourists to escape. As she walked to her apartment, she caught a familiar flash of long dark hair. She slipped Bea's leash up her arm, and sure enough, felt that cold watchfulness. Of course, Deanna. The seed of an idea sprouted in her mind.

She pretended to have not noticed the Investigator and went inside. She locked the door behind her. It was hard enough to deal with OCES, Liam, and Talia all breathing down her neck. But maybe she could get them to distract one another for a bit. She dug through her bag until she found the card Deanna had given her and dialed the number.

"Investigator Parvel," came the cool voice.

"Yes, Investigator. This is Zira."

"Hello, Zira. What can I do for you?"

Deanna was from Quadrant Two, just like Talia. And Talia had pretty much said she owned Quadrant Two law enforcement, so it stood to reason that Deanna was one of hers. If she could send Talia off in the wrong direction long enough, maybe Zira would have enough time to figure out a way off the ship.

Zira allowed a tremor of fear into her voice. "Investigator, I've found myself in a mess. I need to talk to you."

"I can meet you at the station."

"No, I don't think it's safe for me there."

Pause. "I see. Where would you like me to meet you?"

"There's a cafe near my apartment in the Copper District, Platinum Roast. Could you meet me there?"

"Yes. I'll be there as soon as I can."

Zira hung up and headed out of the building to the spongy green path that wound gently through apartments and lift stations starboard to the cafe. The halls were quiet, most folks who lived in her neighborhood would be at work in the Gold and Silver Districts. Deanna would have to pretend she wasn't sitting outside, so that gave her the opportunity to get into the cafe first, grab a cup of coffee, and take a table in the back corner. While she waited, she watched the advertisements flash across the ceiling.

With her phone she could instantaneously pay for and download something to read, watch, or even the music playing over the speakers to listen to later. Or, if she hated what was playing, she could pay for music of her choice to pump through a headset to drown it out, or if she wanted to spend a bit more, she could change the music playing over the speakers entirely.

When she and Marlyn were a new couple, Marlyn would hack systems like that and make restaurants and cafes blast loud, angry, anti-establishment music over the speakers. She smiled at the memory. Zira had loved music in those days. Somehow in the last three years that had changed. It didn't connect anymore the way is used to. Didn't give her that gentle high that helped her rise above the thoughts and emotions around her to revel in the unified message and feelings of a great song.

Maybe, when she went home, she'd turn on some music and see if it moved her again.

The door chimed and Deanna sauntered in. Her boxy suit almost identical to one Zira had last seen her wearing, but a shade of green so dark that it was almost black, and her lipstick was bright purple. Zira waved and Deanna came and sat down without ordering. The barista shot her a dirty look but said nothing.

Zira checked her watch. Deanna had waited, but not very long, confirming her suspicion that she was the one watching her.

"Well, Zira? What did you want to tell me?"

Zira stroked Bea once then let go of his fur, wanting to take in whatever feelings she could from Deanna. Cold calculation and a small, warm flutter of anticipation.

"I had a very disturbing conversation with Talia Heding."

Deanna kept her face blank, but a brush of bitter disappointment scraped against Zira's mind. She didn't care, and wasn't surprised, about her meeting with Talia because she already knew about it. Probably that was as good a confirmation as she was going to get that Deanna was working for her.

"Yeah, she implied that if I don't work with her as a kind of spy, that she might do something to hurt me." Zira allowed her very real fear to make her eyes go wide and hoped Deanna read some surprise in her expression as well. She needed Deanna to think she didn't suspect her ties to Talia or this wouldn't work.

"That is very disturbing. We will of course do everything in our power to keep you safe from criminals and black-mailers."

"And there's more." Zira's heart pounded with nervous excitement. Now she needed to send Talia off after Liam. She acted as though he wasn't a threat to her, but if that were true, she'd have killed him already and been done with their feud.

Deanna tilted her head and waved for her to continue.

"I got a call from Liam Batoc. He thinks that somehow I can help him destroy Talia Heding."

Deanna's excitement reignited. "What does he want you to do?"

"At first he didn't tell me. But earlier today he called and told me that he has someone high up inside OCES working for him who has been investigating stardust. He's planning to try and destroy stardust production or put pressure on OCES to start charging licensing fees for sales. I'm not sure which, it sounds like it depends on how much influence this person can bring to bear. He wants to arrange a meeting between me and his spy so I can Read them and find out if they are being completely honest about what they've learned. Naturally he can't do it himself because he doesn't to attract attention to the informant with his presence. He seemed confident, cocky frankly, that this was going to work, but wanted to make sure that his spy isn't actually a plant from Talia Heding."

"When is this meeting supposed to take place?" Anger and eagerness bubbled from Deanna.

"He didn't say. Just said it would be soon."

"Whenever he arranges it, I want you to go. Read this spy. We need to know who it is and what they know. If they really do know the location of stardust production, that information can't fall into the hands of Liam Batoc, it would start a war between the corps that would be devastating. And, if we have a spy in our midst, we need to know who it is and what their motives are."

"What about Talia Heding?"

Deanna smiled and her delight took on a cold edge of scorn. "If this person has information that would help us bring down her as well then I should say that's a jackpot for you."

Zira nodded. "I suppose that's true."

"Thank you for contacting me, Zira. I'll be in touch."

Deanna stood, strode to the bar, and slid a card over the barista's tip jar on her way out. The barista's glare softened.

Zira stayed at her table until Deanna was out of sight. She released the breath she was holding and drooped into her seat, relieved. Hopefully, Deanna was on her way to pass that information on to Talia, who would turn her laser focus on Liam. With a little prodding, the two of them would be so busy fighting and stabbing each other in the back that she might slip out of this.

She stood and patted her thigh. Bea leapt up from under the table and followed her out the door. As they ambled towards the apartment, he leaned into her, nudging her to the side. Something he often did when they were close to bumping into someone who was radiating particularly volatile emotions. But the walkway was empty. She glanced down at him and he stared up at her with his big brown eyes.

"What?" she asked.

He grunted and nudged her gently again.

She looked to her right and laughed. His favorite toy store, The Golden Fleece. "Alright, you mutt. You've been good."

He wagged furiously when she veered towards the entrance. Inside were rows of children's toys that talked, waved, and sang. The front held the expensive gaming systems and robotics that she doubted had much of a market in this neighborhood but certainly caught the eye and walking through to the more reasonably priced toys with crying kids in tow probably led to a few unwise impulse purchases. In the far back was a section that sold low-tech kids' toys like stuffed animals and balls that could serve for a human or a dog.

The rest of the store smelled sterile, like plastic and chemicals, but back here it smelled like musty fabric and tickled her nose until she sneezed. She preferred the sterile chemicals. But Bea danced, his front paws popping off the ground in tiny, suppressed jumps of glee. She unhooked his leash. "Go on, pick whatever you want."

She wasn't getting paid now, so this was probably a bad idea, but treating Bea to a $10 toy wasn't going to make or break rent, plus it made them both happy.

He trotted back to her side with a red ball and a stuffed emerald-green bird in his teeth.

"I said one toy."

He sat down and whined.

"Oh, fine. You're so spoiled, you know that?"

He trotted after her, tail wagging and toys held in his mouth. The young woman with curly orange-red hair at the register glanced at the leash in Zira's hands and her face hardened. But as soon as she saw Bea, his mouth stuff full of toys trotting happily behind her, she hid her mouth behind her hand and giggled.

"I'm going to need those now." Zira bent down and took the toys from him. He released immediately, but watched her with wide, baleful eyes until she paid and gave them back. Bea trotted at her side out of the store and back to her apartment.

When they stepped out of the elevator, the door to her apartment stood ajar. She stopped and turned back to the elevator, but the door had already closed and headed down. A tall heavily muscled man stepped out from the doorway of her neighbor's apartment. She changed directions and headed toward the emergency stairs. The sound of footsteps and breathing behind her grew closer and she broke into a run.

The door stuck and she yanked it open. Waiting on the other side was a woman with a shock of white-blond hair who filled the doorway with her height and broad, solid body.

Zira turned, but the man was behind her. Bea growled, his hackles raised.

"We're just here to talk to you, Zira," the woman said.

"About what?"

"Mr. Batoc has some questions about your activities today."

The man dropped a heavy, gloved hand on her shoulder and led her forcefully towards her apartment. Inside, another man waited, this one slender and well dressed. The man pushed her to the couch and then he and the woman took up position behind her, the long-bladed knives on their hips shining and visible from the corner of her eye.

"You saw Talia Heding today."

"Yes. I was just about to get in touch with Li – Mr. Batoc." She pulled Bea to sit between her legs and wrapped her arms around his neck protectively.

The thin man folded his hands and sat back, waiting for her to continue.

"She wants me to work for her, just like he thought."

"Good. What did she want you to do?"

No point lying about that part. "She wants me to act as her agent inside OCES. Recruit, pass on information, that kind of thing."

"That was expected. Anything else?"

She swallowed her nerves. If her plan was going to work, she needed Liam to be on high alert, just like Talia. "She has someone on the inside already who is working to bring down Mr. Batoc. She thinks this person is getting close to proving that he's been building and stockpiling projectile weapons."

The man glanced at the two guards over her shoulder. Zira allowed herself a quick flash of the feelings around her. Calm boredom behind her. A flash of fear from the man before her. Was that actually true? She was just leveraging one of the only crimes serious enough to actually get Liam in trouble. Was Liam building projectiles? Actual guns? She knew they'd existed once, they were quite prominent in old stories. But they lived on a spaceship. Such weapons would be madness. Apart from the possibility of a bullet making it through the hull and killing them all, there was complex machinery that kept them all breathing and powered the gravity drive keeping their feet on the ground. But they could also give someone ruthless and fearless enough to risk killing them all absolute power. Liam clearly valued his own life dearly, was he that fearless? She didn't think so, but the man was a gambler. And an arrogant one at that. He truly might think that no one would call his bluff.

"That's utter nonsense. Projectiles are highly, and rightly, illegal. Did she say who she is working with who's trying to prove such an outrageous lie?" the man asked.

"No. But, she wants to arrange a meeting between us. I don't know when."

"I see. This is your new priority, Zira. You must find out who this person is and tell us immediately, do you understand?"

"I do, yes."

"Good. And Zira?"

"Yes?"

"Make sure you keep us better informed of your activities. I don't want to have to come visit you in person like this again. If I do, Mr. Batoc will certainly want to make a more forceful point. Do you understand?"

She nodded and the man shot her a thin-lipped smile as he unfurled from the chair. The two massive guards followed him out. Bea whined and licked her hand with his warm wet tongue.

When her legs stopped shaking enough to stand, she realized his new toys hadn't made it into the apartment.

She peeked her head out the door and saw them in the middle of the landing. She gathered them up and closed and locked the door.

A soft tapping brought Zira out of a light sleep. She yawned and Bea jumped off her lap.

The speaker buzzed. "It's Marlyn."

She went to the door and opened it. Marlyn's unofficial black uniform was still sleek and clean, but her purple spiked hair was starting to droop from a night of sweating and working. She stepped aside to let her in.

Zira led the way into the apartment. "Do you want anything? I don't really have much. There's coffee and whiskey, but it's shitty whiskey."

"Zee, I've been working in the bar all night, I've had more than my share of whiskey. Water would actually be great."

"I have that." Zira retreated to the kitchen, feeling flustered. She filled two glasses and put three cubes of ice in Marlyn's and one in her own.

"Is it okay if I pet Bea? He's making puppy-dog eyes at me," Marlyn called from the other room.

"Yeah, he's off duty right now."

Marlyn giggled, followed by the telltale *thud thud thud* of Bea's whip-fast tail on the coffee table.

Zira took the water to the couch and smiled to see Bea wiggling on his back while Marlyn rubbed his belly. Humor and warmth radiated from Marlyn.

"He likes you. He doesn't let just anybody do that." She set the water down on the table and plopped down on the couch.

Marlyn glanced up and smiled, her real toothsome smile that showed the gap between her front teeth, not the flirtatious smirk she wore at work. It was nice to see it again.

Zira told Marlyn about her day after leaving the Purple Rose and she listened and nodded along.

"God damn, Zee. I see what you're doing. Get Talia and Liam to think the other has aimed OCES right at them and maybe they'll get so distracted with each other that we can slip out."

"That's the idea."

"Do you have enough money for a transport?"

"That remains the biggest problem. Before all this started I maybe had enough to get myself on an Intership Taxi, but not enough for Bea and you. But I'm on unpaid leave for the time being and this place is expensive."

Marlyn looked around and nodded appreciatively. "Nice place like this with no roommates or bugs, I'm betting the owners don't take paper money."

"No, straight from my bank account. Daily. Whether I live here or not. Hell, whether I'm alive or not. Until either my money runs out or my lease ends."

"What a racket."

"It really is. But I couldn't keep living in the Bronze District. OCES doesn't much trust me given my past and that would bring more scrutiny on my neighbors than would be right."

Marlyn sipped her water. "I don't have the money either. Talia takes pretty much all my profit minus a very moderate living allowance."

"Maybe Talia and Liam will kill each other and blow up OCES headquarters while they're at it. Then it won't matter."

Marlyn snorted. "You notice either of us ever being even half that lucky?"

"Suggestions?"

"Well, if you're playing all three sides against each other, you could take Talia up on her offer and see just how much money she's offering."

"I suppose it's not that much riskier than what I'm already doing. She promised a signing bonus, but I have my doubts about her just handing over money."

"You'd be surprised. You might have noticed, but Talia thinks very highly of Readers. The rest of us are dull-witted tools at best."

"I did pick up on that."

"You don't think that though, right?" Marlyn locked eyes with her.

Zira swallowed. It was a seductive thought and one that she'd entertained a few times. "That's ridiculous." She rubbed her temples and sighed. "I understand it, though. I mean, normal people treat me like I'm contagious every day. I can see the appeal of wanting to believe you're better."

Marlyn's eyes softened. "Yeah. I guess I get that, too. I don't think that, you know. I don't believe any of the terrible things people say about Readers. I did maybe, when I was younger. And if I ever said anything back then, when I didn't know... well, it was shitty and I'm sorry."

Zira swallowed a rush of relief mixed with old pain and shame. There had been times when Marlyn had spat curses at mind-eaters, but so had nearly everyone else she'd known in those days. The things she'd said had been mild compared to things she'd been called since then working for OCES, but things that made her shrivel and want to disappear or scrub herself clean from the inside out.

"Thanks." She cleared her throat. "Alright. I guess that's something like a plan. I'll call her in the morning and tell her I'm on board."

"You sure? This is dangerous," Marlyn said.

"Hey now, that's my line. Like you said, doing nothing is more dangerous."

Marlyn yawned and nodded.

"You must be beat. Get some sleep. You can take my bed."

"What about you?"

"Honestly, Bea and I usually sleep out here."

She smiled and warmth rolled off her. "I remember you used to always sleep on the couch until I got home from work. It was cute."

Zira's cheeks warmed and her stomach turned itself in knots.

"Goodnight, Zee."

"Goodnight."

Marlyn disappeared behind the curtain that separated the bedroom from the rest of the unit.

Bea watched her go and glanced back at Zira as if disapproving. Zira stretched out on the couch and Bea curled up in a ball with his tail covering his nose at her feet. She scratched his back and then laid back. Whatever sleepiness she'd felt before Marlyn arrived was gone. The thought of her ex sleeping a few feet away made her heart race and her skin prickle with memories of how Marlyn's soft skin felt against her own.

After an hour, the curtain slid open with a rustle of fabric. Zira pretended to still be asleep and waited for Marlyn to tiptoe through to the bathroom. But she didn't. The footsteps paused in the living room and then moved towards the couch.

"Zee? Are you awake?"

She considered pretending to be asleep, but dismissed it as childish. "Yeah."

Marlyn's warm hand reached under the blanket and entwined with her own fingers. "You don't have to sleep alone if you don't want to."

Zira sat up and was about to ask what she meant when she felt Marlyn's breath on her cheek. She leaned forward a few inches and found her soft lips.

Kissing her felt like coming home.

Chapter 9

Zira's alarm chirped and for a moment, she forgot where she was, and her heart pounded. Marlyn's soft stomach and breasts pressed against her back, and the familiar sound of her almost, but not quite, snoring in her ear took her back to three years ago, before all of this had happened. In sleep, Marlyn's emotions and thoughts were fragmented. Hazy and dreamy and soothing, punctuated by the seeming non-sense imagery of dreams.

But then she remembered that Talia had given her a deadline that was about to run out.

She sat up and silenced the alarm. Marlyn yawned and stretched her arms. "God, it's so early."

"Sorry, we're on deranged crime boss time, not bartender time."

Marlyn snorted a laugh.

Zira rolled over and dug her unofficial phone out from the pockets of the pants she'd worn the day before and dialed the number on the card Talia had given her. It rang once and beeped. No answer and no outgoing message.

"Um. It's Zira. About what we talked about yesterday. I'm in. Call me back."

"Now what?"

"I guess we wait. Are you hungry?"

"Starving."

Zira slipped on a robe and dropped the phone into a pocket.

"Hey, where you going?"

"To make breakfast."

Marlyn stood and the sheets slipped off her plump, naked body. Zira stopped for a long moment and stared in appreciation. Marlyn wiggled her finger, beckoning, and Zira obliged.

"If we're going to do something so cosmically, probably fatally, recklessly stupid, I want a good morning kiss."

Zira laughed and kissed her back.

Marlyn pulled her in close and slapped her ass. "Okay. Now feed me."

Zira gave her one last quick kiss and went to the kitchen and dug through the cabinets and refrigerator for something to throw together. At last she settled on pancakes. While the batter sizzled on the small stove, she poured food into Bea's bowl. He wagged his tail as he ate.

She flipped the pancakes onto plates and carried them back to the still warm bed. She handed one to Marlyn and climbed under the blankets. As she took a bite, there was a knock on the door.

"Damn." Zira set her plate down on the nightstand. Bea looked up from his breakfast and followed her to the door, crumbs of food still dusting his lips. She looked at the camera and saw Deanna looking impatient.

"Stay here." Zira closed the curtain, hiding Marlyn from view and then opened the door.

"Investigator. What can I do for you?"

"Come with me." Her voice was cool and her emotions hard to identify. They seemed somehow dulled, as if from behind a thick blanket.

"Where are we going?"

Deanna raised one arched eyebrow. "I think you know the answer to that."

No more pretending they didn't both know who she worked for, it seemed. "Alright. Could you wait in the living room while I get dressed?"

"Of course." Deanna strode into the apartment and stood watchful and statuesque in front of the couch.

Zira ducked behind the bedroom curtain. Marlyn was already dressed and handed her a pair of black pants with red stitching and a red shirt. She quickly shimmied into the clothes and ran her hands through her hair.

"Good luck," Marlyn mouthed and gave her a quick kiss.

She smiled and tried to look confident and fearless so Marlyn didn't see the dread building in her chest that matched the fear she felt radiating from Marlyn.

She grabbed Bea's leash from the counter and clicked it to the collar. "All right."

He turned suddenly serious, the wagging and playful look gone from his eyes, as he transitioned seamlessly from her goofy friend to her staunch ally and support dog.

Deanna's mouth curled in an unfriendly smile. "Would Marlyn like to join us?"

Zira's heart dropped. "I don't know what..."

Deanna crossed her arms and gave her a scornful look.

"No. She won't join us." But Deanna's point was made. They knew their bargaining chip had become more valuable.

Deanna led her and Bea out of the apartment to a waiting private transport and waved for her to get in first.

The inside was covered in supple pineapple leather and smelled of liquor and cigars. Soft, instrumental music played and the windows darkened until they were opaque. On the ceiling gentle, warm lights turned on. Solar lights. The kind that provided vitamin D and encouraged serotonin instead of merely providing light to see by or to draw attention to a casino. Everyone received a small time-ration for the sunrooms to minimize depression, but to light the inside of your transport with them was decadent.

"Where are we going?"

Deanna didn't answer and the music got louder making conversation difficult. Zira sat back and tried to still her racing heart by stroking Bea's soft fur and listening to the exquisite music.

At last they stopped, and the windows turned transparent once again. A man in a black suit opened her door and nodded to Deanna. "I'll take her from here."

Deanna lowered her eyes and nodded. "Thank you, Reader Itolous."

Zira climbed out of the car and followed Itolous. He hit a buzzer and a door hissed open. As she walked past him, he stepped forward too quickly and bumped into her.

"Sorry," Itolous murmured.

She waved him off and gazed at the scene before her. Inside was pitch black except for splashes of glowing purple. It took time for her eyes to adjust, but when they did, she saw that she was in a garden. The ground was some kind of black dirt; it collected on the buckles of her boots in strange, almost tree-like shapes. She reached down and flicked it off. It was cold and metallic under her fingers and as soon as one layer was removed, a new one collected. The dirt was magnetic. Massive purple flowers shaped like bells burst from the strange magnetic dirt and inside each, a glowing orb of light the color of starlight. It looked like a place where fairies should live.

"What is this place?"

"I regret, Reader Zira, I can't explain quite yet. That is for Madame Talia to tell you. But please, do not touch the flowers. They are very delicate and very important."

The vaguely cult-like vibe surrounding Talia's residence was unsettling.

Magnetic dirt crunched under foot as she walked, and she was careful to avoid the glowing flowers. For all she knew they might burn or explode when touched. At the end of the garden smiling people milled about in large, open rooms lined by glowing blue seams in the floor. On the wall were switches that would raise the walls for privacy, but now, all were down. In each room was a large, luxurious bed with silk sheets. In the center was a kitchen with gray and black marble counters where a tall man with a mustache chopped actual fresh vegetables. A handful of people wandered about the compound talking while others sat in plush velvet chairs with e-readers or goggles over their face, lost in games or movies.

It was the most open space Zira had ever seen.

Talia strode through her wall-less palace, wearing a tailored purple suit with a silk turquoise scarf wrapped around her neck. "Zira, welcome."

"Thanks."

"This is my home. One I share with many other Readers, so I'm sure you can understand why you were brought here in such secrecy."

She nodded.

"Let me give you a tour." Talia smiled, her face more relaxed, almost open and friendly.

"Sure, thanks."

Talia led her through the open rooms, introducing her to other Readers who smiled and welcomed her enthusiastically. When they were done, Talia led her back to the kitchen and the chef placed fresh coffee, cream, ripe strawberries, and scones shiny with butter on a plate in front of them.

"Well, what do you think?" Talia poured a generous amount of cream into her coffee and took a bite of scone. Her face was relaxed and smiling. She seemed excited to be showing off her home to someone new.

Zira considered avoiding the food. She remembered her mother telling her stories about the land of fairies. You weren't supposed to eat or drink or you'd be trapped there forever. But, the smell of butter and cinnamon made her stomach growl and remind her that her breakfast had been interrupted. She grabbed a scone. Butter moistened her lips and the sugared outside crunched beneath her teeth before giving way to the warm, soft center.

"This is delicious."

Talia gave an appreciative nod to the chef. "I'm glad you like it. And the rest?"

"It's beautiful. What is that growing in the garden?"

"Everyone who lives here is a Reader. It's quiet. There are no unwanted feelings and thoughts bouncing around, everyone is taken care of. You don't even need a dog to stay sane, although everyone is more than welcome to have one," she added quickly, looking at Bea.

Zira glanced around the huge open space. Aside from Bea, there were no other support dogs to be seen. "I can definitely see that being relaxing at the end of the day."

The chef glanced at her and then immediately averted his eyes.

"I don't expect any of them to go out and deal with Books." Talia spat her own personal epithet for non-Readers as if it pained her to even contemplate their existence.

"They don't ever leave here?"

"Why should they? They have food, company, entertainment. Everything they could want."

"I see." So, they were very well-kept prisoners. Charming.

"When your work with OCES is over, you will live here too."

"Excuse me?"

Talia laughed. "Of course. It's not safe for people like us out there. Even walking around is enough to drive you mad, even if everyone around you doesn't actively hate you."

"And if I don't want to live here?"

Talia touched her arm. "I don't see why you wouldn't want to live here. But some people don't. And that's just fine."

Even if she couldn't Read anyone in this room, she could still feel tension in the air. Talia had already told her that she had other, less pleasant uses for Readers. What had that meant? And why did she avoid her question about the garden?

"Now, let's discuss business. Deanna tells me that Liam Batoc may have his own agent within OCES. One who thinks they know something about stardust and where it's produced. I'm not very worried about his threat to levy licensing fees, that idea would easily be erased from anyone's mind in OCES. But Liam is a daring, arrogant, brute. He could try to destroy production on his own."

Zira nodded. "Yes. I see now that I'm not safe, and I think you have my interests at heart more than OCES, and certainly more than Liam Batoc."

"I'm glad to hear that. Although I hope, in time, you'll see that allying with me is more than merely the best option available."

"I hope so, too. At the moment though, being on unpaid leave has me in a tough position. I'm close to losing my apartment and I can't live here while I'm working for OCES still."

Talia's face tightened. Zira's response was clearly not what she'd wanted. She'd probably expected her to be impressed or excited. And when she'd been twenty, mostly alone and angry at the world, she probably would have been won over by a beautiful cage.

"I mean, this place is amazing. What you've done here is really incredible." Zira swallowed the lump of fear in her throat and pushed on. "You mentioned –"

"A signing bonus. Yes, you'll get it."

"When?"

"As soon as we agree to terms."

"And what are the terms?"

"Your handler," she sneered as she said the word, "I want you to Read him. Don't take anything besides his memory of his encounter with you. It's quite likely you'll need to take memories from him often and even if you're careful it starts to take a toll. So, do try to be cautious or else we'll have to break in a new one sooner than I'd like."

"What should I be looking for?"

"This is just reconnaissance you could say. A chance to prove yourself. Check to see if he has ties to Batoc or any hidden agendas we should know about. And if he happens to know anything about this mysterious Investigator looking into my business, that would be a happy bonus."

Zira's mouth dried. "I have no objection to doing that, but I don't know when or how I'm going to be alone with him and get close enough to do that."

"Not to worry. Deanna will arrange the opportunity, you will just have to be bold enough to take advantage when it comes."

Deanna once again darkened the windows so that Zira couldn't see out on their trip home. She tried to pay attention to the movement of the vehicle so she had some sense of where they were going, but it felt as though they were driving in circles, and she gave up trying to figure out their route.

The transport stopped and the windows turned transparent. Her apartment complex stood just outside.

"Be prepared. I'll have you brought in to the station tomorrow, so make sure you're home."

"I will." Zira slid out and the door hissed shut behind her.

She didn't turn to see, but she felt Deanna's eyes on her back as she climbed the steps to her building and went inside. Would Marlyn still be here? She half expected to walk and find out she'd disappeared like a dream. Or maybe come to her senses and run screaming back to her bar.

She opened the door and lightly tapped Bea's forehead. "Okay." Her entire body seemed to warm with happiness when she saw Marlyn sitting in her chair.

Bea trotted from her side and bumped his forehead against Marlyn's hand to encourage her to rub his ears, then he disappeared under the table, grunting in his battle with his new stuffed bird.

"How did it go?" Marlyn asked.

"Weird." Zira told her what she'd seen and about Talia's offer.

Marlyn shook her head. "She's fucking awful, but she is damn cunning."

"Yeah. She really pushed me into a corner." Zira slipped off her jacket and tossed it on the chair.

"What are you going to do?"

"What she wants. At least for now. We need that money and she loves Readers. I don't think she'll kill me on a whim. Which is more than I can say for Liam or OCES."

Marlyn nodded. "And she's powerful enough to at least make them think twice before trying to hurt you."

"That too. Though, she wouldn't hesitate to hurt you or Bea or anyone else in my vicinity if she thought it would tighten her hold on me."

Marlyn took Zira's hand and kissed her palm. "Don't

worry about me. I've been tangling with her longer than you have. And between us, we'll keep Bea safe. I promise."

Grateful that Marlyn didn't dismiss her fears about Bea, she watched him wrestle with the stuffed bird. His playful sweetness made her more frightened for him. None of this was his fault. If she got him killed she didn't know what she would do. She needed him. He was the only family, the only friend, and the only source of kindness she'd had for three years.

Marlyn interrupted her reverie. "While you were gone, I did some thinking."

"Uh oh."

Marlyn winked. "Now, now. Show a little trust. I've been thinking about the way Talia takes money from us poor stooges. The way it works is that every time I swipe someone's chip to pay for a drink, the money goes straight into an account she set up. At the end of each week, she sends me the agreed upon amount for business expenses plus ten percent and then the rest goes to her, disappearing into whatever accounts she has set up to hide her money. Nobody else talks about it because nobody wants her to suck out every happy memory they've ever had and leaving them a weeping puddle of sorrow and trauma. Which is something she did to the owner of the Stratosphere. But I'm positive the other businesses she's squeezing do the same. If I could reroute that money into an account of our choosing, we wouldn't have to worry about whatever she means by a 'signing bonus.' We'd have more than enough for an Intership Taxi."

Zira shook her head. "You're good, Mar, but the only people who would know her system would be the businesses she's blackmailing. She'd just send a Reader out to find out which one."

"Then I do it right before we're ready to leave."

"It's too dangerous."

"So is staying here."

She was right, of course. If they didn't get off this ship, Zira would end up dead or living in Talia's cult palace. Marlyn would, at best, be held as insurance against Zira leaving, at worst, she'd be killed by Liam Batoc, OCES, or even Talia wanting to rid Zira of outside ties.

"Maybe, *maybe* you're right. But, let's call it our backup plan. Talia just giving me the money is safer for both of us."

"Agreed."

Zira's phone chirped. She dug through her pockets and pulled out both phones. Her official line.

"Hello?" she said.

"Zira. I'm sorry to say, your father has been arrested," Deanna said.

"Excuse me?"

"For hiding a Reader from OCES. You should come down to the station, right away."

She hung up and buried her head in her hands.

"What's up?"

"My dad has been arrested."

"Talia?"

"That's my guess. To give me reason to go to OCES headquarters."

"And to make sure you stay in line."

"Probably that too. Though, I don't why she thinks that would work. She must know I hate him."

"I have no doubt she does know that. But she also probably spotted you're too nice a person to let your own father be turned into a drone. Especially for the crime of not turning you in sooner."

Zira groaned. "You're right. Goddammit. Fine. I'll go see what I can do."

Marlyn kissed her. "Be safe."

"You too."

Chapter 10

Zira walked through the main floor of OCES. Officers in their matching yellow and black uniforms and Investigators in cheap suits with gold badges stared at her and Bea. The usual levels of suspicion and low-level resentment that usually hummed about the room whenever she made an appearance were amplified and pressed against her despite the leash connecting her to Bea. She touched his fur to silence the rush of emotions while they waited for Deanna and Paulson.

Paulson appeared first. He strode down the hallway, the gold badge on the lapel of his ill-fitting black jacket askew. Without a word, he waved for her to follow him into interrogation room four.

Already seated, and looking poised as ever, was Deanna. Paulson sat beside her and pointed at the chair across the table. "Sit."

The chair was nailed to the floor to prevent a suspect from

using it as a weapon, and she had to squeeze between it and the table.

"As you've no doubt heard, we've arrested your father, Quentin, for failing to report that his child was a Reader to the proper authorities," Deanna said.

Zira nodded. "He did turn me in, so I'm not sure what we're doing here."

Paulson tapped a thick folder on the table. "It took him more than thirty-years to do so and when he did, he failed to mention that he was your father and was paid a substantial reward. OCES provides rewards to citizens who go above and beyond, not to parents who shirked the law for thirty-years."

"Well, my father and I are not close. I can't say I feel a powerful need to defend him, but I doubt he even knew what I was. He wasn't around much when I was a kid."

"Heartbreaking," Paulson said, his voice held a mocking edge.

Deanna leaned across the table and whispered something to him. Paulson nodded and she stood and left the room.

"Where is Inspector Parvel going?"

"She thought you and I should talk alone. Handler to Reader, and I agreed."

Zira glanced up at the camera pointed at the table and saw the light blink off. Apparently, this was the opportunity Deanna was creating for her. She let go of Bea's leash, being careful that it didn't make a sound when it hit the floor.

What she found made cold dread squirm through her insides. Glee bounced off of him like shards of glass. He was happy. She frightened him and he was happy she was going to hurt. There was something more going on here.

Zira glanced at the cameras again and saw that they were still dark.

"Now, where to begin?" He turned his computer towards her and displayed the image of a man with an underbite like a bulldog and nose that had been broken so many times that it looked like lumpy clay.

"Who is that?"

"Why don't you tell me?"

"I've never seen him before." Careful to keep the gesture as subtle as possible, she rested her right hand on the table.

"His name is Danyal Landry and I believe he had something to do with the death of Anna Farrow, also known as Anna Lytle."

"Why would I know him?"

"Because he was blackmailing you. You found out where Anna Farrow lived from her brother and told your accomplice."

"That's absurd. I've never seen that man before and there's nothing for him to blackmail me with."

"Inspector Parvel believes that you found more than you're saying. You took too much time in Farrow's head for what you reported."

"I know what she believes and she's wrong. This isn't a science and it can't be calculated and measured like one."

He looked down at his tablet and swiped to another picture. While his attention was on the screen, she walked her hand across the table until she was as close as she could get without stretching visibly.

"Fine. How about this woman?" A picture of Marlyn flashed on the screen. It was an old picture; her hair was shaved and the remaining fuzz dyed bright pink.

Marlyn was in her apartment right now. Her DNA would be all of the scanners and would be in the records from her old apartment going back years, so there was no point in lying. "My ex-girlfriend. Marlyn."

"Ex?"

"We met up again recently. It's not anything serious at this point." She shrugged.

"See, a pattern is starting emerge here. Your... associates all have ties to the same person. Talia Heding."

She didn't have to fake confusion. "What?"

"Your girlfriend was on our radar as someone who helped hide a Reader and kept company with Curtis Farrow. On a hunch, I ran DNA scans of her bar and what do you know, but it turns out, he was there not two months ago. More recently, Danyal has been a regular visitor and word is, he is a bribe collector for Talia Heding. Which leads me to believe your girlfriend works for her. The constant here, is you. You're surrounded by people who work for Talia Heding and people who are neck deep in Anna Farrow's murder. That leads me to believe that you're working for her as well."

"You're wrong. I'm not. And if Marlyn is paying money to Talia, that's her own business. Being indebted to someone is not a crime, is it?"

He glared across the table. "It is if she's indebted to Talia for erasing her liquor licensing debt."

She held his gaze for a long time. It didn't make sense. Why was Paulson so keen to go after Talia? OCES left the corps alone. They didn't have the resources to go after Talia, not really. OCES Investigators and Officers liked their jobs because they were safe. They got to throw their weight around and scare people, get some respect in a world where working class people didn't have much of it, and collect bribes. Going up against Talia for real would be dangerous. Only if someone really got them worked up, really got them scared and angry would they take that risk.

When he looked back down at his tablet, Zira lunged the last few inches across the table and rested her hand atop his. His body jolted and went rigid and his eyes lost focus.

Flies. So many flies. They blanketed his face until his features were hidden and still more poured from his mouth, a vibrating waterfall of wings, legs, and fuzzy bodies. They swarmed about his head, stretching their proboscis to reach him, growing fat on the fear and rage, violence and suffering that leaked from his mind.

She was only supposed to take a casual look around, but overwhelmed by curiosity, she followed his memories down until she saw the night of Anna's murder and delved inside. He'd left work to meet a host who worked at the Silver Spoon. She'd come onto him while he was drinking alone after losing a bundle at cards. He had been in such a hurry to meet her, that when he glanced in the backseat he realized he'd left a tablet he'd found in a safe in Curtis Farrow's house in his transport. He decided to let it wait until tomorrow. After all, Farrow was already a drone, what would another day matter?

He returned to his transport after spending the night alone, enraged that he'd been stood up. Glass from his shattered transport windows crunched under his feet and the backseat was empty. Given the circumstances, he didn't report it and told himself it didn't matter. Farrow was an open and shut case and there probably hadn't been anything important on the tablet.

His radio buzzed alerting him that a homicide had occurred. He shoved his lingering fear about the lost evidence from his mind.

Zira almost let go of his hand when the memory of Anna's slack face, slit throat, and blood-soaked covers filled his brain.

When he found out who she was, he panicked. If it was discovered that the evidence stolen from his car led someone here, he was done. Even if he couldn't prove definitively that the murderer didn't get the address from that tablet, he'd lose his job. He'd have to face his own Reader with her creepy eyes and perpetual smirk that made him think she knew things about him that she shouldn't. He stepped outside to think and ran into a stocky man with a face that bore the lumps and scars of someone who had seen more than a few fights.

"Looks like you're in some trouble, friend," the man said.

"What would you know about it?"

"I know you're not gonna find who offed the lady. All that evidence is gonna just go poof." The man waved his arms like a magician with his wand.

"And if it doesn't?"

"If it don't your mates are gonna find some pictures of you leaving with evidence so you could meet some no-show floozy. I hear they give bad Enforcers like you over to the mind eaters to determine just how corrupt you are.

And I got the sense, yours don't like you much. Probably won't be much of you left when she's done."

Paulson shuddered. He was trapped. "Fine. What do you want me to do?"

"Well, seems to me, easiest thing to do would be to find out someone else killed the woman. That way your mates stop looking, too."

"You have someone in mind?"

"I do. Think real hard. Who should have known about the woman and who isn't real well liked?"

"Zira?" Paulson asked?

The man pantomimed shooting a pistol. "Bullseye. Send up the mind eater, nobody's gonna care."

"She's the only one in this quadrant."

"All the better."

A wilting sense of defeat combined with a guilty excitement to be rid of Zira worming about his stomach, Paulson nodded.

He went back to headquarters and researched Readers who had been executed. He found the file for a Reader in Quadrant One who had been executed seven years ago. The Reader let a serial murderer walk out of an interrogation cleared of all suspicion because the Reader's dog ate all the memories of the murders. The Reader covered up what the dog was doing and when it was found out, both were shot full of poison and dissected. The doc who did the cutting wrote an influential paper about the chemical processes that linked a Reader to their dog. It was perfect.

Paulson used the case as a model and created the groundwork for a case against Zira and Bea. He would tie

her to Talia Heding. Just enough that everybody would jump to the proper conclusions about motive. Just enough that they'd be afraid she was ripping memories from his coworker's minds and reporting back to Talia. It was a fine line for him to walk. Push too hard, and he'd risk forcing Talia to get involved and no one wanted to cross that bitch. She was even scarier than Zira.

Deanna's appearance and expertise put Paulson on the sideline of the investigation and had made his plan more difficult, but he continued to push it forward, whispering to his fellow Investigators about Zira and Talia and hoping he could get Deanna to latch onto the theory for him.

If successful, his plan was a death sentence for both her and Bea. She wanted to slam his face into the wall. She wanted to kick him until his ribs broke. To set her and Bea up to be executed because he was a lazy, inept, corrupt bigot was infuriating.

But she couldn't do that. She couldn't eat all of his memories of his plan either. Not yet. If he walked out of this office a drone, everyone would know she'd done it and the end result would be the same injection of poison. She had to let him go and trust that Deanna would keep her safe from further scrutiny.

She swallowed down his memory of a flash of fear when he saw her hand snake towards him and sat back.

He sat looking bewildered for a second, blinked, and looked back down as his tablet.

The door opened and Deanna appeared. Had she been behind the blackmail? Had Talia set her up to force her into this corner to work for her? If so, it was about time to loosen the knot so she didn't end up dead.

Deanna glanced at her and Zira nodded subtly.

"Investigator Paulson, you know it's against protocol to interrogate a Reader alone. Luckily for you, I kept an eye on the camera to see that you weren't compromised."

He blinked like a man who was startled from a deep sleep. "But you –"

"No, keep your mouth shut. I expected more professionalism when I came here. But I will not report your lapse in judgment to your superiors this time. I trust it won't happen again." Deanna's voice was sharp and authoritative. Despite Zira's mistrust of the corrupt Investigator, she wanted to cheer seeing the confused, chastised look on Paulson's face.

The door slammed open. "Investigators," a young officer shouted.

"What is it, Officer?" Deanna asked.

"You better come."

Deanna and Paulson glanced at one another and stood. Without a word, they left, locking Zira and Bea in the interrogation room.

Zira reached down and picked up Bea's leash and clicked it back onto her wrist. She rubbed his ears and tried to ignore the grating *click clack click clack* of the clock on the wall.

Forty-five minutes passed and she started to wonder if she'd been forgotten, but then the door opened. Paulson strode inside, his face hard and angry while Deanna's mouth was pursed in an expression of enraged shock.

Deanna sat down while Paulson continued to lurk in the open door.

"Zira, I'm very sorry, but your father was found dead."

Her stomach clenched and she felt as though she'd been slapped. "What?"

"He's dead, Zira. I'm sorry, we don't know what happened." Deanna bit her lip.

"What, he had a heart attack?"

"No. He was found suffocated."

Zira's body was cold with shock. She didn't know if she was sad, angry, scared, or even relieved. "Suffocated," she repeated.

"Yes. He was alone in his cell, so we don't have an obvious suspect."

"Liam Batoc," Zira spat.

"Why do you say that?" Paulson asked.

Deanna gave a single, sharp shake of her head and Zira bit back her response.

"I understand that you are upset, Zira. But Liam Batoc is a business owner and pillar of this ship. It would be unwise to make unfounded accusations." Deanna's voice was crisp and professional, but she couldn't help but spit out her boss's rival's name.

"I haven't seen my dad in a long time. But I think he works—worked for Liam," Zira muttered.

"Thank you, that is worth looking into," Deanna said. "Now, you should go home. I don't think it would be appropriate to continue these questions given the tragic circumstances."

Paulson looked about to protest, but a sharp look from Deanna cut him off and he closed his mouth.

"Do you want me to call you a private transport?" Deanna asked.

Zira shook her head, still feeling numb, and walked out into the bustling crowd and flashing lights of the Golden Nova.

When Zira arrived at home, there was a note taped to her door that simply said, "I'm still waiting." Liam. He'd warned her that he'd kill her father if she didn't take down Talia. But this was just vicious, he couldn't possibly have expected her to do it that fast. She ripped the note off the door, crumpled it, and went inside.

Marlyn stood at the kitchen sink, doing dishes. When she heard the door, she turned. "Hey, you made it. I was just doing some anxiety cleaning." She pointed at the damp, glistening counters then scrutinized Zira's face. "What's wrong?"

"My dad is dead. I think Liam Batoc had him killed to motivate me." Zira started to laugh and Marlyn stared at her. The laughter erupted from somewhere deep inside and she couldn't stop it. It spilled out and doubled her over. Her stomach muscles ached and she recognized that the laughter sound frantic and unhinged, but couldn't stop.

Marlyn touched her arm and Bea snuffled her hand, but Zira drew away from them both and curled into a ball on the floor. The laughter changed and suddenly there were tears in her eyes and she was crying. Bea rested his head on her knee and looked up at her with big, brown eyes. His eyes were so nonjudgmental and trusting that she cried harder. She was going to get him killed too if she didn't figure something out.

Marlyn slid down beside her. When the fit of giggles and sobs died down, Marlyn wrapped an arm around her and murmured nonsense words of comfort.

Zira wiped her eyes and took mouthfuls of air. "I'm okay now."

"I'm so sorry," Marlyn said.

Zira shook her head. "I didn't even like him. Even without the betrayal and the complete disinterest in me and my mom, he was a petty, cowardly, poor excuse for a person. He'd have sold his own mother for a lottery ticket that someone promised him was lucky."

Marlyn rubbed her back. "I know. But he was your dad and that's not so easy to let go."

"I guess." Zira leaned her head against the door and closed her eyes. After her outburst, she felt hollow and sad, but calm.

Bea sat up and licked the salt from her cheek and she stroked his long fur. "Thanks. Both of you."

"Let me get you some water and something to eat. Then you get some sleep if you can and we'll worry about what's next tomorrow. Okay?"

"Yeah. That sounds good. Thanks, Mar. I'm really glad you're here."

Marlyn set a glass of water and a sandwich down on the table. "I don't mean to add to everything, but I found something while you were gone."

Zira took a sip and waved for her to continue.

Marlyn picked up a piece of paper from the counter and straightened it. "Help. She's killing us," was scrawled in black.

"Where did that come from?"

"It was laying by the chair. I was guessing it came from your coat pocket. One of Talia's pet Readers?"

Zira stared at the scribbled noted and replayed the events at the compound in her mind. "It must have been. There was a Reader named Itolous who bumped into me. I think he was the only person who touched me besides Talia."

Marlyn turned the note and shook her head. "Those poor people. I don't know what we can do for them, though. Stardust isn't illegal."

"Murder, blackmailing, and kidnapping is."

"Yeah, for most of us. But OCES won't go after Talia, she's too powerful. Legal doesn't apply to corps."

"We have enough of our own problems without trying to mount a rescue mission," Zira said, feeling guilty as the words left her mouth.

"I know. I just wish we could help them somehow." Marlyn sighed and laid the note on the coffee table in the center of the living room where it lay, the edges curling up in a way that looked both defeated and accusing.

Chapter 11

Zira's phone dinged and dragged her out of a fitful sleep. She looked at the screen through bleary eyes. A message from Deanna.

"Thank you for your help, Reader Zira. My superiors are grateful and will do as agreed."

Marlyn lay behind her, spooned against her back and looked over her shoulder at the message. "What does that mean?"

"I think that means I'm getting paid today."

"We should be getting ready to go then."

"Anything you still need to pack?"

"I'll need to stop by home while you're out to grab a few things. Oh!" Marlyn jumped up and Bea grunted and gazed her mournfully at being dislodged from his spot on her feet.

"What?"

"We can't forget this." She picked up Bea's red rope and

his new ball and stuffed bird. His ears perked, but even his favorite toys couldn't get him off the couch when he was sleepy.

Zira warmed. "Thank you. Bea would be so sad without those."

"So, I'll make sure to keep our bags on hand. You do whatever you need today to make sure we don't look suspicious, and I'll meet you at the transport bay."

"I still have to make sure OCES isn't able to respond when they get the alert that I'm trying to leave."

"Right. Well, then they have to be busy."

"I have a plan. I don't think it's a good one though. Liam, Talia, and OCES all believe I'm working for them. If there were a major fight at the Silver Spoon between Liam and Talia's people, OCES would have to respond en masse. Especially if they were under the impression that Liam might bring projectiles into the mix."

"I see what you're thinking. You tip off Liam that Talia's on her way. How do you get Talia there? Or, at least enough of her people for a solid distraction?"

"I tell her that Liam found out where her compound is through his OCES spies and is coming for her stardust supply."

"That would do it. They all have to trust you enough to believe that though."

"There's the crux of the issue."

Zira's phone dinged with another message. It was from her landlord. She opened the message to see a statement. She scanned it, prepared for a negative balance and an angry warning about eviction. But, instead, it said that not only was she caught up on her rent, but that she was paid up for the next three months. At the bottom, it thanked her for also enrolling in the building's food delivery program and she should look forward to her first delivery in three days. She stared at the statement in confusion until it dawned on her. She groaned.

Marlyn sat up straight. "What's the matter?"

"Talia is too fucking smart."

"Uh oh. What?"

"My signing bonus turned out to be having my rent paid and food covered for the next three months."

"Shit."

"Yeah."

"Plan B, then," Marlyn said.

"No."

"No what?"

"I don't want you risking yourself like that. Not after –"

"We talked about it. We agreed. I'm sorry about your dad and I know you're scared for me, but unless you have another idea for how to get enough money to get off this ship, this is the plan." Her voice was warm, but firm.

Bea tensed and cocked his head. He'd adapted to Marlyn's presence surprisingly well, but argument made him concerned and confused about what he should do to provide comfort.

"Fuck fuck fuck. Okay. Fine. But, if we're going to do this, we need to be prepared to run if it doesn't work." Zira stood up from the table and paced. Bea jumped off the couch and walked close by her side.

"I agree. How's this, if this goes badly, we both make a run for Quadrant Three. Not ideal, but the big corps don't have as much of a presence there," Marlyn said.

"Yeah, because there's nothing there but drone-populated factories."

"So, no one there will be able to care much about us. We'll regroup and figure out something else."

"That's not how drones work. They see someone who isn't supposed to be there, they get confused and start screaming. That is if we can avoid the DNA scanners."

"It won't even come to that. This is going to work."

Zira groaned. "Fine. It's a shitty plan, but it's the only one we have."

A soft chirping interrupted their conversation. Zira glanced at her phone. "Shit. It's Deanna."

Marlyn grimaced.

Zira picked up the phone. "Good morning, Deanna. What can I do for you?"

"I'll be there to pick you up in thirty minutes. Make sure you're dressed."

"What?" Zira asked. But the line clicked, and Deanna was gone.

Marlyn raised an eyebrow.

"She just said she's going to pick me up. Not big on giving polite notice of her kidnappings."

"You did what she asked, so Talia probably wants to give you your next assignment."

"I hope that's all. I'm not sure what we're going to do if she forces me to live in her cult palace."

Marlyn snorted. "Don't worry, if that happens I'll hunt you down even if I have to walk every inch of this ship to find it. You go do that and I'll get my equipment so I can start figuring out what I need to do to get into her account. We'll want to time our escape for two days from now. That's right before Talia moves the money out so it'll be at its maximum."

Zira sighed in resignation. "Alright, you win. But be careful, okay?"

Marlyn kissed her. "I won't promise careful. But I will promise to be smart."

Zira laughed. "Best I can hope for. And try to stay away from anyone who works for Liam. You and Bea are on his list after my dad. I'll give him a call, see if I can't buy us some more time."

"I will. You be careful with Talia."

Zira smiled what she hoped was a reassuring smile, but with her puffy eyes and the knot of tension in her chest, she feared she looked more unsettling. She fed Bea while she slipped into fresh clothes and cleaned up. She dialed Liam, but got no answer so settled for leaving him a message that just said, "I'm close. Give me time."

Her phone beeped. "I'm outside," read the message.

She grabbed her bag and went out to the transport where Deanna waited. The ride was again pleasant with soothing music, glowing sun lamps, and blackened windows.

"I'm sorry about your father," Deanna said.

Zira shrugged, not wanting to process her feelings with the person who probably arranged to have him arrested in the first place.

They rode once again in a long, twisting, circling path so that Zira couldn't even begin to guess which end of the quadrant they were in or even if they were still in Quadrant Four at all. At last they stopped, and a tall man once again greeted them in his expensively cut black suit and blank expression. For a moment she thought it was Itolous, they looked so similar, but this man had slicked-back black hair with no wave and a much squarer jaw.

"Reader Zira." He nodded.

Zira nodded back, looped Bea's leash around her wrist two extra times, and followed him.

A woman in a tailored navy suit knelt in the magnetic dirt and carefully squeezed drops of pink-tinged liquid into the bell-shaped purple blooms from a pipette.

Talia came out of the compound to greet them. "Reader Zira. Thank you so much for coming back so soon." Her face was open and smiling as if having a friend over for tea.

Zira plastered a fake smile on her face and played along. "Thank you for the invitation."

"Come inside, let's talk." Talia waved her inside.

Again, the silent chef prepared food. This time he placed small, flaky croissants in front of them. Zira picked one up and bit through buttery bread and into rich, creamy dark chocolate. She moaned involuntarily. It was incredible. Talia looked pleased at her enjoyment.

"Deanna tells me you Read your handler as agreed. What did you find out?"

Zira considered lying, but there was a very real possibility that Talia was the one who sent Danyal after Paulson to make Zira's situation desperate enough to work for her. Lying would give her away. So, she told her what she'd seen, omitting her own speculations about Danyal's likely employer.

Talia nodded and made noises to indicate her interest. "It is disturbing your handler is trying to link you to me as if that were something criminal. Stardust is completely legal, of course. He'll have to be dealt with. And certainly this Danyal isn't working alone. I expect Liam Batoc is behind it, as well as your father's murder."

"Undoubtedly," Zira said.

The chef caught her eye for a second, perhaps picking up on the insincerity of her tone and she thought for certain she saw him nod.

"I trust you found your signing bonus more than adequate? You did say you were having a problem making rent while on suspension."

"Very much so, thank you. You're very generous."

Talia smiled and Zira was reminded of a praying mantis. "I'm generous to my friends."

"Then I'm glad we're friends."

"I hope we stay that way." Talia's voice held an edge of warning.

"I plan on it."

"Good. You've shown you have the skills I need and can be reliable. I'd like to show you a bit more of my operation."

"Uh sure, I'd like that." Zira wanted nothing less. She wanted to take Bea and get them both out of this web of blackmail and cult-like insularity and run as far as they could.

"Good." Talia led her outside and knelt next to one of the glowing purple flowers. "Do you know what this is?"

"Beyond it being a flower, no, I don't. I've never seen anything like it or even like the soil."

"Look closer. I guarantee you have seen something like it before."

Zira frowned and looked inside the bloom. She knew nothing about plants, as having space to grow anything was a luxury. But this one had a stem inside that was so black it seemed to swallow the light around it. Dotting it were glowing white, red, blue, and yellow lights that appeared to be its pollen. As she stared at it, she was reminded of standing in front of one of the hull windows watching the sea of stars in the inky black.

"Stardust," she murmured.

"That's right." Talia watched her face intently as if waiting for something.

"How did you find them? Or figure out how to make them?"

"I'll tell you that story a bit later. I hope you understand, Zira, that in showing you this, it means I trust you. Stardust isn't illegal, but it is coveted. But more than that, it is a threat to all of us."

"A threat? I don't understand."

"I would be very angry if someone I trusted were to betray that trust. Wouldn't you?"

Zira swallowed. Talia had a way of speaking where she sounded earnest, friendly, conspiratorial even, but underneath every word was a threat sharp as a scalpel.

"Come on, we have more to see."

Zira followed her back inside. Talia flipped open a switch pad on the wall of the kitchen. A previously invisible door, smooth and identical to the wall around it, hissed and popped open. Talia beckoned her down a staircase so narrow that Bea was forced to walk behind her instead of at her side. He whined softly as an unpleasant smell wafted up the stairs. The sterile scent of bleach mixed with something sickly sweet and musky. It brought back memories of visiting her mother in an overcrowded hospice in her final days, as she died much too young of illnesses gone too long untreated. It smelled like death.

At the bottom of the stairs was a laboratory. Glass bottles and shiny steel implements glittered. Several gurneys were lined up, most empty, but a body lay in one. A familiar body. Itolous. His head rested above a hole in the gurney and a tube snaked through, empty now, but attached to a vial half-full of clear, blood-tinged fluid. Fuck. What the hell was this?

"What happened to him? Is he...dead?" Zira tried to hide the disgust in her voice.

"Yes. I'm afraid Itolous proved to be untrustworthy."

Her mouth dried, afraid she knew about the note he'd slipped her. "How?"

"He tried to leave with another Reader. His sister. I was sad to lose him, I was very interested in them. So far, no one has identified how our ability is inherited, or even if it is. Families with one Reader are likely to have more, but I've yet to find a Reader who gave birth to a Reader child. And I encourage sexual activity here in our little paradise. But, for whatever reason, no one has conceived."

Zira had a sickening feeling that Talia's idea of encouraging sex was more of an edict.

"And if you don't much fancy any of your community members, we do have access to the best equipment and techniques medical science has to offer. There is no reason for you to be physically intimate with a man to create a child. In fact, I find that science can be much more reliable in that regard."

A shudder ran up her spine. "What happened to the other one?"

"I'm sorry, the other one?"

"His sister."

"She's just fine. She joined me first and it seems Itolous here thought it was his duty to rescue her from her own choices."

"What are you doing to him? What is that?" She gestured to the tubes snaking out from his neck.

"That is how we make stardust. The flowers you see outside are powerful opiates, but when combined with just a single drop of cerebrospinal fluid from a Reader, they give the user the most glorious visions and sense of euphoria. I can even create special strains by using, or combining, the willingly provided fluid of a living Reader who has eaten memories and feelings of certain qualities."

That explained where the rumors about Talia buying memories came from. Not a rumor at all. "Does that hurt?"

"Quite a lot. Although, a small price to pay to be able to live comfortably among our own kind. It takes power and money to be free on the Golden Nova."

"I can't argue with that."

"I don't show you this to scare you, but because I show all new members of our little community. This is our home and our family and there are consequences for betraying your family."

Talia's eyes were hard, and her pursed mouth made her cheekbones jut even harder against her skin, so she appeared to be all angles.

Bea whined. The tension and the smell of death was probably making him anxious. Zira rubbed his ears. "It's okay, Bea. You're okay."

Talia eyed Bea. It was then Zira realized that Talia's own

support dog didn't seem to accompany her inside the compound. She couldn't conceive of not having Bea with her all the time. Even when she didn't need his ability to quiet the emotions around her, she still wanted him with her and knew he felt the same. The bond between Reader and support dog was a profound one. It made her trust Talia even less that she didn't see her own dog in the same way.

"How are you able to keep your supply up if it requires a Reader to die?" Zira asked.

"It doesn't really require a Reader's death. I can, and do, work with only the fluid of a living Reader. In fact, stardust is more potent that way. I kept Itolous alive for hours and he provided quite a bit of fluid before he died, but eventually draining that much fluid is fatal. However, even in death those who betray their family can still be useful. I can harvest all of their cerebrospinal fluid in a way I can't with the living. I can produce enough low-quality stardust from one body to meet current demand for a year. It also allows me to supply consumers at different price levels and cater to different experience preferences."

Talia strolled to the steel counter and gestured at a line of sealed jars. Each one filled with black liquid and shimmering with trapped stars and topped with a different colored lid. "The cheapest is stardust derived strictly from the dead or dying." She gestured at a row of red lidded bottles. Then she held up one with a blue lid. "There are of course fine distinctions in between, but in the middle, I use a base created from someone like Itolous and mix it with fluid derived from a living volunteer to create a more potent, long-lasting, and complex high. At the highest end is the pure fluid of a living Reader who has been fed a steady stream of sexual memories, childhood experiences, or more generally, memories and feelings of joy or comfort. There are some less popular specialty strains as well. Some like to use stardust to enhance creativity or to cater to a love of fear, so there is a small market for those created with darker or more complex emotions and memories."

Zira's stomach churned. "Impressive."

Talia's lips twisted in a mean smile. "I think so."

"How did you even figure out how to do this?"

"I did this for us. For Readers. I wanted to build a community where we could live together in safety and to do that, I needed money. I used the skills I had in botany and medicine to design something that would be in high demand but that only we can make. We have to control this trade. If we don't, some greedy non-Reader will do it. And then, we're all just a drug supply to them. It's bad enough that law enforcement conscripts us into their service. If they knew about stardust, they'd breed us like livestock."

A tough stance from a woman who had offered to artificially inseminate her on their third meeting. Zira forced her eyes away from Itolous' open, milky eyes. "You're probably right."

"Come, let's go back upstairs. It's so dark down here."

Zira patted Bea's back and followed Talia up the stairs and back to the garden.

Talia perched on an ornate black metal bench and patted the spot next to her. Zira sat and Bea squeezed between her legs and turned so he could watch outward protectively.

"I'm sure you're wondering what's next for you." Talia watched as a woman plucked some of the purple blooms, putting each in its own sealed jar.

"I am."

"I want your remaining time in OCES to be as efficient and short as possible. You should only have to live among them until you've recruited enough key people that we can let money and fear do the rest of the work."

"That's not so easily done when I'm under suspicion for fucking up an investigation."

"Indeed. And to clear up that bit of messiness, I need to be rid of Liam Batoc. I'm quite certain he's behind your trouble."

Zira looked away so that her face didn't give away her certainty that Talia was behind the vast majority of her legal problems. "I thought you didn't expect anything so ambitious from me quite yet."

"Oh, I don't. I only expect you to play a part in my little play."

"What part is that?"

"You're going to confess to Deanna and your handler that when you Read Curtis Farrow, you saw in his mind that he worked for Liam Batoc. Based on what you saw, you were understandably afraid for your life if you told them what you'd seen."

"You think they'll arrest him based on my say-so?"

"Not at all, but combined with Deanna's considerable influence and your handler's fear of her turning the investigation into Anna Lytle's death towards OCES and his own conduct, I think he will come around."

"You think that'll work? Liam Batoc is pretty well known for bribing his way out of legal trouble."

"I know it won't work. But it will be enough to have him brought in. And when he comes, he'll have to be alone and unarmed. Deanna will make sure he doesn't leave alive."

Zira pretended to stare into the distance as if mulling something over. "There's something you ought to know."

Talia raised one arched eyebrow.

"I have reason to suspect that Liam Batoc may be working to build projectile weapons with the intention of coming here."

Talia stared at her, searching deep into her eyes. "Does he know where this compound is?"

Zira shook her head. "Not yet. But he's looking."

"And how did you come to learn this?"

"It's a hunch, but a good one. I told you he tried to blackmail me into going after you. Well, some of his goons showed up at my apartment the other day. I sensed fear and I knew they weren't afraid of me. Something Liam was doing scared them. There isn't much that has real consequences for people like Liam Batoc or those who work for him. I threw out that suggestion to see how they reacted and they were terrified."

Talia's brow furrowed. "That's very interesting. Even more reason for me to be rid of him as soon as possible. But I will have to make sure to have my own people watching the building when Deanna has him brought in. I wouldn't want them panicking and staging an ill-conceived rescue operation. Will you do your part?"

"Yes. As long as I have your word that you have my back."

"Of course. You're my family now and you don't betray family."

Zira nodded and stroked Bea's ears. Guilt worried at her heart. Not for Talia, she could hang as far as she was concerned, but for the people who lived here. Clearly some of them were prisoners and some of them were at least somewhat willing, but if this worked, Talia would either be dead, enraged, or on the run. What would happen to them? What if someone else really did get a hold of stardust?

Talia smiled down at Bea, but her eyes were cold. "You two have a special bond."

She tightened her grip on Bea, feeling protective. "Yes."

"That's so important out there." She waved vaguely towards the outside.

"Not in here?"

"Why would it be? There's no one in here to torment you with their endless thoughts and feelings. Not even Deanna is allowed past the door."

"I see. You did say support dogs were allowed."

Talia waved. "Of course. Why wouldn't they be? You don't need them, but they do no harm. But, on that note, Deanna tells me you've renewed your relationship with Marlyn."

Zira said nothing.

"That's fine, of course. If you're going to be involved with someone out there, I'd rather it be one of my people. Though you must know she can't be allowed in here and I would rather no lovestruck Books start sniffing around trying to find you when you leave. Take whatever comfort you need from her during the next few days, but it would unkind, and unwise of you to let her think your relationship is a lasting one."

She didn't speak until her anger was sufficiently under control as to not color her voice. "I understand."

Talia patted her knee and Zira fought the urge to scoot out of reach. "Good. I think this has been a very productive day for both of us. You're going to fit in very well here. Deanna is waiting outside to take you to your apartment. Do take care of yourself these next few days, Reader Zira."

She stood and nodded to Talia. "Until next time." She hurried through the garden and out the door as quickly as she dared, not wanting to seem too eager to escape Talia's presence and her macabre garden.

Chapter 12

Zira climbed the steps to her building and entered the door code. The door clicked open.

"Zira." Paulson's voice came from behind her.

She groaned and turned to see him and Deanna side-by-side with identical stern expressions.

"Yes?"

"You're under arrest for obstruction of justice. Come with us."

Zira glanced up at the window of her apartment. This was happening too fast. She needed to talk to Marlyn. She needed to know that the plan had changed. Shit.

"Zira, turn around. Don't make this harder than it has to be," Deanna said.

She pressed her eyes closed and breathed deep, then turned and climbed back down the stairs. Deanna took Bea's leash from her and she felt panic start to fog her mind. She jerked her arms, reaching for him.

"Bea will ride with you in the car," Deanna assured her.

Zira's mind cleared, but her hands still shook. Paulson's unfiltered glee washed over her and dwarfed the cool, quiet feeling of satisfaction trickling from Deanna.

He bent her arms behind her, and the cuffs closed with an electronic beep. He grabbed her, his hands covered in heavy gloves to protect him from her ability, and led her to a waiting transport. She should have spotted it right away. OCES transports were obvious, even when they were supposed to be blending in, like this one. Windows a shade darker than normal and absent any fashionable splashes of glittering, metallic paint.

Paulson pushed her into the back and Bea hopped in behind her and rested his head on her knee with a soft whine. The door snicked shut.

Deanna climbed into the passenger seat and turned to her, giving her a terse, affirmative nod before Paulson climbed behind the controls. They sped through the glittering corridors, past the Silver Spoon and the Sunfish, and came to the dim OCES garage.

With Paulson on one side and Deanna, still leading Bea, on the other, she walked into the building. Without Bea, she felt the pings of hostility and low-key fear that radiated like a thin layer of fog off the Officers and Investigators who filled the office like buzzing honeybees. Some looked up at her. A few smirked, but most averted their eyes as if afraid she'd suck down their memories from across the room. A flash of anger and hatred at the hypocrisy of forcing someone they despised to work for them burned in her chest.

They led her to an open interrogation room.

"Give me the dog," Paulson said.

"I'll take the dog. You should stay here, you're her Handler after all," Deanna said.

Paulson glanced at Zira and a wave of cold fear swept the room. Apparently after Reading him he was even more frightened of her, even if he didn't remember the details.

"I got the dog." He ripped the leash from Deanna's hands and turned. But Bea didn't move. He sat fast, all forty pounds of him refusing to budge.

Paulson yanked him so hard that he slid across the slick floor, but still he refused to leave Zira.

"Goddammit, don't drag him like that, you'll hurt him," Zira yelled.

Deanna put a hand up. "Paulson. That's a support dog. Let his handler give him the proper commands to go with you."

"Fine. Do whatever it is you do." He glared at Zira.

"Where are you taking him?" she asked.

"Bea will be fine. He just has to undergo an examination," Deanna said. Her voice was cool and even.

Paulson made a motion as if to start dragging him again.

"Okay." Zira raised her cuffed hands and snapped her fingers. "Okay. I'll see you soon Bea."

Bea cringed and Zira's heart ached, but he followed Paulson out, his tail clamped tight to his haunches.

Deanna glanced up at the camera. The light blinked and turned off. "I'm sorry about this. But it's going to be okay. Just do what you're supposed to, and I'll get you out."

"What about Bea?" Her voice was high pitched and frantic, but she couldn't control it.

"Do what you need to, and he'll be fine."

It was hard to Read Deanna's emotions. They were so muted and sparse. But she felt a flutter of something. Guilt. Fear. And she was sure that Deanna was lying.

The door opened and Paulson returned.

"Zira was just about to tell me something, I asked her to wait for you."

"Well?" he asked.

Zira calculated. She could refuse to go along with Talia's plan in hopes that would give her leverage to get Bea back. But probably that would put him in more danger. She would follow the plan and point the finger at Liam. Talia's people would be outside waiting to see that his people didn't interfere. If all went according to plan it would be a massive fight and she could slip out. Maybe. And maybe she'd find her way back to Marlyn who would have no idea this was happening right now because nothing ever went according to plan.

"Zira?" Deanna prompted.

"I lied before. About what I found in Curtis Farrow's head," she said.

Delight and satisfaction rolled off Paulson. From Deanna she only got quiet. Who had Deanna had been before Talia? It wasn't just memories that Talia was taking, it was bits of personality. Zira had brushed past a lot of minds in her life, and no one was as even and cold as Deanna. It felt like Talia had siphoned off all the fire and sharp edges of Deanna's mind to create a highly capable and inconspicuous drone.

"Curtis Farrow was working for Liam Batoc. I didn't want to say anything because, well, I saw in Curtis' head what Liam did to people who crossed him and I was afraid. He's–"

she added a tremor to her voice, "Liam is building projectiles. Guns. I saw it in Curtis' brain. I saw him shoot someone. It was horrible."

"Is that everything?" Paulson asked.

She looked down at her hands and nodded. "That's everything."

"What about Curtis' client list?" Deanna asked.

"What about it?" The question came as a surprise. She'd almost forgotten that Curtis and that fucking list was how this had all started.

Deanna looked at Paulson, her glance significant. "You were right."

He nodded. "It's the dog."

"What's the dog?" Zira asked, panic began to constrict her chest.

Deanna smiled kindly. "We believe you, Zira. I know this isn't going to be easy to hear, but Bea has been taking some of the things you Read."

"He damn well is not."

"I'm sorry, it's true. The scans we did when you were here before were conclusive. The only question was whether you were aware he was doing it. And if you were, if you were hiding what he was doing or directing him to do it. I feel very certain that you didn't know." Deanna gave her a look of pity that didn't match that feeling of cold determination pouring off her.

"What does that mean?"

"As soon as we get a veterinarian in here, the dog will be put to sleep and a necropsy performed to see how we can prevent this in the future. You'll be assigned a new support dog. As for you, concealing evidence is still a crime, but given the mitigating circumstances, you will not be sentenced. However, for the next two years your pay will be reduced forty percent and you'll be under house arrest when you're not working," Paulson said. Glee and relief poured from him. Even if he wasn't getting rid of Zira entirely, he had her diminished, contained, and he thought he was free. But he was just a petty, vicious pawn. Talia had set them all up.

"You can't do this," Zira said.

They ignored her.

"I'll have Batoc brought in for questioning," Paulson said.

"You think it'll stick?" Deanna asked.

"Nothing has yet, but we have a Reader again. She can't Read Batoc, but she can Read everyone in his employ." He pointed at Zira.

"If you think I'm going to work for you after you kill my dog –"

Paulson shrugged. "I'll think you'll do what you have to do, like the rest of us. I'll go make the calls." He left her alone with Deanna.

"Zira, I am sorry. This was the only way to take suspicion off of you. I don't think you realize how close you were to being executed along with Bea."

"Without Bea, there's no deal," Zira said.

Deanna sighed. "Be reasonable. You've done what we need. There's no going back." She stood and walked around Zira towards the door.

As she passed, Zira spotted a small patch of skin that peeked out above Deanna's glove where her sleeve had bunched at the wrist. She reached up, her cuffs clanging together, and touched the exposed skin. Deanna froze.

Inside Deanna's head was a surgically precise labyrinth of memories. Black memory flies buzzed and hummed, swarming fragments of bloody memories that littered her mind like the remains of a shattered mirror. In the spaces between were large, empty rooms filled with white noise. Talia's unmistakable touch as a Reader.

A recent memory floated to the surface. Talia and Deanna sitting in the black-windowed transport, OCES building looming in front of the windshield.

"You understand what you need to do?"

Deanna nodded. "Liam will die and when Reader Zira's dog is euthanized, I will see to it her request for a new one is denied."

"Good. Then she'll join us. I will not have one of us living out here with filth."

"No, it is unacceptable."

"Go. If Liam's people try to rescue him, our people will handle them."

"What about OCES?"

Talia shrugged. "Liam's people will start it and we'll be the heroes who kept OCES from being completely destroyed. When it's all over, OCES will be weaker and more pliant and Liam will be dealt with."

Deanna nodded and reached for the door.

"Wait. One more thing."

She stopped, her hand on the door.

Talia reached over. Panic flooded Deanna's mind, but she sat still as Talia's fingers touched her cheek. The path of her memories opened into another, empty room.

Deanna turned and nodded to Talia, her mind now cool and placid. She knew Talia had taken something from her, but was unable to feel what she no longer remembered. But Zira could feel a distinctive shallowing of her memories and personality. Talia didn't take anything entirely, only skimmed a bit of everything, preventing Deanna from building a solid enough foundation of memories and experiences to be independent or rebellious. Who had Deanna been before Talia?She wondered again what Deanna might have been like before Talia. Before constantly having her memories and personality pruned like some hideous bonsai. She had a moment of sympathy for the Investigator.

It didn't matter now, whoever she had been, that person was gone and this one was prepared to kill Zira's best friend. Zira didn't have Talia's scalpel-like skill, so she pulled everything. She sucked down the fly-coated memories of the uncountable times she'd killed someone for Talia to force a Reader into a state of desperation, or to protect Talia and her 'community.' She drank the mundane nights of scouring records and DNA scans to locate unknown Readers. The bulldog-faced man who had taken the evidence from Paulson's car smiled at Deanna, thanking her for the tip that would rid him of, what he believed to the be the only person left who knew his old name, the one that was wanted by Liam Batoc for successfully cheating in one of his casinos.

When she was done, there was nothing at all left of Deanna except a shell of flesh and built-in instincts. Zira released her. Deanna stood and stared, confused and lost.

Zira cleared her throat and Deanna stared at her blankly.

"You have a card in your back left pocket, can you take it out?" Zira asked, keeping her voice as friendly as she could.

Deanna nodded and reached into her pocket, pulling out a white card with a blue barcode on the side. She stared at it, puzzled.

Zira held up with handcuffed wrists. "You see that red light on the left cuff? Tap the card to it."

With no reason not to, Deanna did as she was told, and Zira's cuffs snapped open and dropped to the floor.

"Good," Zira smiled, and Deanna imitated her.

"Now this is going to be a little harder. I want you to go out that door, turn right, and go inside the room labeled with the number four. You got that?"

Deanna smiled again. "Got that."

"Two men will come soon. Tell the pale one to leave you alone for five minutes. The other man will have on hand-cuffs just like I did. Use that card just how I showed you on him, okay?"

"Okay."

"Last thing, and it's very important. Take this," she pointed to the red-handled knife strapped to Deanna's hip, "and give it to him."

Deanna smiled, her eyes wide and eager to please. She opened the door and turned right as instructed.

Zira peered out the door to watch. She hoped Deanna could follow all those instructions, but at the very least, her bizarre behavior should be a distraction. Paulson would be in there soon with Liam Batoc, assuming he found him, and she hoped more than anything that he found him, or else this half-baked plan of hers wasn't going to work.

She glanced at the clock and prayed that Bea was still alive.

At last Paulson appeared with a straight-backed and proud Liam Batoc walking before him. They turned into the interrogation room and Zira stepped out into the hall. She hurried, opening each door looking for Bea and listening for his distinctive whine over the soft hum of voices drifting from the lobby.

He may have already been euthanized. She might be too late. Her chest tightened. How could she forgive herself if Bea died because of her?

She heard a bark and broke into a run. A yip came from her right and she slammed the door open.

Bea was alone. Leather straps held him down on a steel table. His brown eyes were wide with stress and his pink tongue lolled to the side. She undid the straps as fast as her trembling fingers would allow.

"I'm so sorry." She rubbed his ears and hugged him. He snuffled her hair and licked her sweaty neck.

"Time to get out of here." She lifted him off the table with a grunt, grabbed his leash, and shoved it in her pocket.

As she stepped out of the room, someone began to scream for help. Liam must have made his move. The air filled with shouts and the thudding of feet. A black and gold uniformed officer went flying across the hallway, a knife buried in his chest while an Investigator in a too-large gray suit waved a knife at another Investigator. Chaos was erupting. Liam must have some people on the payroll willing to defend him.

This was her chance. If she boarded a transport, no one would be here to respond to the flag on her DNA scan. She patted her thigh and she and Bea ran. Alarms blared and screams followed them. A loud crack reverberated through the halls and she clapped her hands over her ears as she threw herself out the door.

Outside, black and gold uniformed Officers exchanged beatings and knife thrusts with black and silver clad guards from Liam's casino. One of them held a long weapon cradled against her shoulder that roared when the trigger was pulled. The weapon spat sparks and bullets and blew a hole the size of a fist in an Investigator's chest. Zira had been right. Liam really was building projectiles. It was fucking madness. Definitely time to get off this ship before someone used it to put a hole clear through the hull.

Looming behind the melee, wearing subtle, expertly tailored suits, was Talia's militia.

Talia's people raised long silver blades and raced towards Liam's. The woman with the gun fired at them, but her weapon, while powerful, was slow to reload and Talia's people fell on her. Blades rising and falling with a burst of blood.

No longer pinned by the gun-woman, OCES officers rallied. Grunts, screams, and thuds filled the air, and everything smelled of smoke and blood. For one horrible moment, Zira lost her grip on Bea and the flood of terror and bloodlust left her reeling and insensate on the ground.

Someone grabbed tight to her hand and the rush of feelings quieted as she was dragged across the slick floor. She looked up to see Bea, her wrist in his mouth, digging in with his back legs, dragging her slowly. She pulled herself up to her knees and squirmed, careful to keep her hand wrapped in his fur, until she was hidden behind a trash bin and a little away from the fighting.

A transport hummed to a stop in front of her. Her heart pounded. Talia must have caught them. She crouched and braced for an attack.

The door clicked open and Marlyn's grinning face popped out. "Get in."

Zira was too stunned to move.

"Now!" Marlyn shouted.

Bea nudged her in the back and she raced forward, threw open the door to the back seat and climbed inside. For a long agonizing moment, she had to release Bea and the flood of terror and pain pressed against her, choking her.

But then, he was there. Pressed against her side and his tail thumping as he greeted Marlyn.

"I don't suppose you got the money to get us the hell off this ship?" Zira gasped.

Marlyn smiled and nodded. "I did. I also saw you get arrested, so I pretended to be you and tipped off Liam's people that they should get down here and rescue their boss."

"You are brilliant. Let's go."

She took off, transport skimming along the surface, up to tracks snaking across the ceiling, and towards the Intership Taxi bay.

Zira hugged Bea and stroked his fur, taking in much needed comfort. She flashed on Itolous's dead face and the unnamed chef's warning glance.

"I only wish there was something I could do for those people still trapped in Talia's creepy cult compound."

"They'll be okay."

"I don't see how. Unless Talia shows up to the fight and gets killed. Which I doubt. She'll be far away giving orders."

Marlyn smirked. "I did something."

Suddenly nervous, Zira sat up. "What did you do?"

"Well, when I figured out how to get at the money Talia's been stealing from all of us, I stumbled on a few of the accounts linked to it."

"Mar, how much money did you take?"

"Everything I could find. I don't think Talia is going to have the power or influence to keep anyone on her payroll or to force those people to stay if they don't want to. I have no doubt she'll be back on her feet again, she's a clever woman, but that assumes those people don't use the opportunity to exact some of their own justice."

"That was an incredibly stupid thing to do. And you're a genius. I love you and I'm so glad you did it."

Marlyn laughed and they pulled up in front of the transport bay and jumped out. They strolled to the ticket counter, barely able to control their laughter and excitement.

"Where to?" the agent asked.

"This transport go to the Oasis?" Zira asked.

He nodded. "I spent my last vacation there. It's a good escape from all the glitter and hustle here on the Golden Nova. You have to do a little work, help them grow food and purify water. But, if you're not an asshole they'll show you a good time."

"They okay with dogs?" Marlyn asked.

"Oh yeah. They're one of the few ships that allow animals. As long as you account for them in your contribution to food production, of course."

"Perfect," Zira said.

"How long you planning to stay and what's your purpose in going?" he asked.

"A week and pleasure?" Marlyn smiled and leaned in flirtatiously.

Zira refrained from rolling her eyes. Unsubtle though Marlyn was, it had the desired effect. He blushed and entered her answers with suddenly clumsy fingers and did not ask follow-up questions.

When they were entered into the system, he waved them forward through the scanner. It hummed as it checked for weapons and they both opened their mouths for the required DNA swab. Zira held her breath when the agent frowned at his screen. After a moment, he shrugged. "Looks like you're good to go. Bay seven."

Zira scanned the signs until she saw a bright red '7.' Beneath it waited a small gray shuttle. The pilot waved at them and opened the hatch. She rested one hand on Bea's back and held Marlyn's hand in the other. Together, they climbed into the cool shuttle and buckled into their seats. Bea curled up between Zira's feet and was soon snoring.

A distant clanging of alarms made Zira's chest clench and her breath caught in her throat. At the same time, the transport began to hum and rise slowly off the ground. They flew through the docking bay doors of the Golden Nova, into the dark, star speckled black.

She squeezed Marlyn's hand tight and waited for the call to turn the shuttle around, but when the Oasis' green, tube-shaped hull filled the window, it still hadn't come. The doors opened and the transport landed with a sudden jolt.

"Enjoy your visit," the automated pilot said.

Together they stepped out of the shuttle into a world of green. Plants covered the ground and trees heavy with fruit towered above filling the air with the scent of apples. Zira crouched to rub Bea's ears and plant a kiss on his furry forehead. Marlyn pulled her to her feet and wrapped her arms tight around her waist and lifted Zira an inch off the ground and they spun around laughing. Bea joined in, running circles around them, wagging, and barking playfully, trying to find a way to wedge himself in between them.

A door opposite them hissed open and a tall man she could only describe as 'thick' from his lush, graying hair down to his dirt caked work boots stepped through. His smile was warm and unguarded in way that made her smile back reflexively.

"Welcome to the Oasis, my name is Marco." His voice was as familiar as an old friend's. The voice that had beckoned her to come here for so many years.

"We're um seeking refuge," Zira managed to say.

He glanced at Bea, understanding and sympathy softened his smile, but it lost none of its warmth. "You are welcome here." He waved them forward.

She gazed over at Marlyn who took her hand and squeezed it, then down at Bea who watched her eagerly for instruction.

"Let's go," Zira said.

Together, they followed.

END

LEIGH HARLEN is a queer, trans non-binary writer of horror and other dark speculative fiction who lives and works in Seattle. Their debut novella, *Queens of Noise* (Neon Hemlock Press), and their short fiction collection, *Blood Like Garnets* (TKO Studios), are available everywhere books are sold.

You can find links to their work at leighharlen.com and follow them on Twitter @LeighHarlen for updates on future publications.

Dancing Star
Press

Dancing Star Press is an independent publisher based in Lansing, Michigan. Our mission is to publish speculative fiction that shows that not only can monsters be defeated, but so can oppressive governments and other forms of social control. We believe in finding hope in the apocalypse, joy in a dystopia, and people and peoples finding their power.

Check out our other titles and leave a comment or review on your favorite social media platform.